Also by Michael Northrop

Gentlemen

Trapped

Plunked

Rotten

SURROUNDED BY

SHARKS

MICHAEL NORTHROP

SCHOLASTIC PRESS | NEW YORK

Library of Congress Cataloging-in-Publication Data

Northrop, Michael, author.
Surrounded by sharks / by Michael Northrop. — First edition.
     pages cm
Summary: On the first day of vacation thirteen-year-old Davey Tsering wakes up early, slips out of his family's hotel room without telling anyone, and heads for the beach and a swim in the warm Floridian waters — and a fateful meeting with a shark.
1. Sharks — Juvenile fiction. 2. Missing children — Juvenile fiction. 3. Families — Florida — Juvenile fiction. 4. Swimming — Juvenile fiction. 5. Florida — Juvenile fiction. [1. Sharks — Fiction. 2 . Swimming — Fiction. 3. Survival — Fiction. 4. Rescues — Fiction. 5. Florida — Fiction.] I. Title.
PZ7.N8185Su 2014
813.6 — dc23
2013045351

ISBN 978-0-545-61545-7

10 9 8 7 6 5 4 3 2 1   14 15 16 17 18

Printed in the U.S.A.   23
First edition, June 2014
Book design by Phil Falco

For my agent, Sara Crowe,
and my editor, Anamika Bhatnagar,
who have kept me afloat in some very perilous seas

PART ONE

CARRIED AWAY

1

Davey Tsering opened his eyes and looked up at an unfamiliar, cream-colored ceiling. He'd slept fitfully on a steel-framed canvas cot, and his body felt a little like he'd just fallen down a mountain. He heard his family before he saw them. His dad was snoring loudly and his younger brother was echoing him like a smaller version of the same revving engine. Davey groaned softly and turned to look around the overcrowded hotel room.

He saw his mom and dad, Pamela and Tam, lying next to each other on one of the room's two double beds. His mom's face was turned down in a grim frown as she slept. Davey peered at the alarm clock on the night table between the two beds. He squinted, but it was too far away for him to read the little glowing numbers. He carefully reached down to the floor for his glasses. The little cot was noisy, and the last thing he wanted was to wake someone up and have company.

He put his glasses on and everything in the room became a little clearer. It wasn't an improvement. There was drool at the corner of his dad's mouth, and his mom was balanced precariously on the edge of the bed.

Davey's younger brother was splayed out in the next bed, the one that was supposed to be Davey's tomorrow night. Davey looked at him for a few moments. He was surprised by how young he looked lying there, and how peaceful. He still looked like the little kid who used to follow Davey around everywhere. But Davey wasn't fooled. He knew that as soon as Brandon woke up, he'd become "Brando." That's what he liked to be called now. Now that he'd turned into a Class-A pain in the neck, now that he'd started arguing with their parents. Like those two didn't argue enough already.

Davey couldn't imagine what that would sound like in this little room. And who needed imagination? He was sure he'd find out before the week was over. He took a deep breath and regretted it immediately. The room was slightly but unmistakably funky. Four people had been in here all night, sleeping, snoring, drooling, and . . . *Oh no,* thought Davey. *Oh Dear Lord . . . Had someone been farting?*

Another breath, this one quick and cautious, confirmed his fear. He assumed it was Brando, but there was no way to be sure. Was it his dad? His *mom*? It was too horrible to think about.

Finally, he remembered why he'd put his glasses on. He looked at the clock: 6:47. *That's it?* he thought. *That's it?* It would be hours until everyone was awake and ready to get moving. He knew what they'd say: "We're on vacation. Let us sleep."

He had to get out. Thirteen and a half was too old to be stuffed into a room with his entire family. One day in, and he already needed a vacation from this vacation.

Slowly, very slowly, he reached down and pulled the thin hotel blanket off his body. His heart started beating faster. If either of his parents woke up, they'd stop him. If his brother woke up, he'd want to come, too. He had to be quiet. Spy quiet, ninja quiet. Ninja-spy quiet.

He pushed his feet slowly over the side and cringed as the cot creaked under his shifting weight. He glanced over at the beds: no movement. He reached out and put his left hand on the windowsill, taking some of the weight off the cot. In one quick, smooth — well, kind of smooth — movement, he stood up.

Davey had slept in a T-shirt and his swim trunks because . . . well, basically because his brother had. If pajamas are too babyish for your younger brother, they are, by extension, too babyish for you. And he had to admit it was a pretty solid plan. His swim trunks were the one thing he could wash himself as the week went on, just by going in the water. They were in the Florida Keys, after all. The Internet described this place as "a sunny tropical paradise with white sand beaches and crystal-blue water." It didn't seem like paradise so far — and it definitely didn't smell like it — but Davey was 100 percent sure the March weather here was going to be better than it had been in Ohio.

Still, he wasn't really a beach person. He was skinny, and he wouldn't call himself nerdy, exactly, but he did like his fantasy books. He leaned down and silently pawed through the little pile of paperbacks he'd set up next to the cot. All the books except one were by J. R. R. Tolkien. Davey was such a big fan that he knew what all the initials stood for. And the one book that wasn't by John Ronald Reuel Tolkien was by his son.

Davey made his selection: *The Silmarillion*. The bookstore lady had told him it was "for serious Tolkien fans only," and so it was his new favorite. He stuffed a few other essentials in the white-mesh pocket of his swim trunks and surveyed the path ahead. He had to walk right by the beds — why on earth had he set up the cot by the window instead of the door?

He walked carefully, minefield-style. The carpet was thick and easily absorbed his weight. Halfway across the room, he heard someone turn over. He knew it was his brother before he even looked — his parents had no room for such large maneuvers. He looked back slowly and was relieved to see Brando in a slightly different position but still just as asleep. The shifting of his blankets had revealed something else, though. Brando was definitely the one polluting the atmosphere. In a way it was a relief.

Davey saw a sliver of morning sunlight through a gap in the curtains. That was his goal. He needed to reach it. He needed to get to a sunny, warm place that didn't sound like dueling chain saws and wasn't contaminated by the burrito grande his brother had eaten at the airport. He turned back toward the door and kept going. He was past the beds now. A few more tense steps and he was at the door.

He pressed down on the handle with slow, even pressure. He knew there would be a click. The question was how loud.

Click.

Not too loud. He didn't hear anything behind him and didn't turn to look. He was too close to his goal. He pushed the door open and quickly stepped through.

In open ocean approximately four miles to the southwest, a very different individual was also up early. Although "up early" wasn't exactly accurate in this case. It had been up all night. It had been up all of its life. But now, in the fresh light of morning, it was on the hunt.

Galeocerdo cuvier. The tiger shark. The distinctive stripes that earned the species its name had faded as this one reached adulthood, but there was a second reason for the name. The sea tiger was at least as fearsome a predator as a tiger on land. It was a massive, muscular brute of a fish. It was sometimes called the man-eater shark, but that wasn't entirely accurate, either. It would eat anything, from sea snakes to sick whales to discarded lunch boxes.

As the sun speared through the warm top layer of the ocean, all of the shark's senses were alive. Its eyes scanned the water as its ears listened for rhythms. It smelled the water constantly with powerful nostrils that had nothing to do with breathing, had no other job. If you were in the water a thousand yards away, it could taste you already. It could tell if you had a sunburn. But it was doing something else, as well.

Small jelly-filled pores along the shark's head were alive to any electrical charges in the water. With them, the shark could sense the tiny charge given off by the muscles of a fish as it flicked its tail. It could sense the vast humming of an ocean current. With a threshold of around five one-billionths of a volt, it could sense nearly anything that moved down here. And that's how it knew it was close.

It had been on the trail all night, gliding patiently through the water. It wasn't sure at first: a faint smell, and far off. And even when it knew — *blood* — it still wasn't willing to expend much energy. The sea was vast and hungry. Food was often gone by the time the shark arrived. The body would be gone, even the scraps, leaving it with nothing but the smell and the knowledge that it was once again too late.

But not today. Its prey was just up ahead. The broken rhythm of an injured animal swimming rang through its senses like a church bell:

Whump-whump-wahamp-*whump* . . .
Whump-whump-wahamp-*whump* . . .
Whump-whump-wahamp-*whump* . . .

The shark could see it up ahead now. It was a loggerhead sea turtle, a rich feast of fat and muscle if the shark could catch it. And there was something wrong with it. One of its flippers was injured. Yes, the shark could see that now. It could see it and smell it and feel it and sense it and taste it.

It could've been hurt by a fishing net or another shark. It could've been anything out here, but it didn't matter now. After all those miles of slow, patient swimming, the shark had closed to within a few dozen yards. The turtle knew it was there now and swam harder.

Whump-whump-wahamp-*whump-whump-whump*-wahamp-*whump*

The effort came to nothing. The tiger shark exploded through the water, closing the distance almost instantly with an impressive burst of speed. And then it was on the turtle and feeding. Its powerful jaws clamped down on the injured flipper. Dozens of broad, backward-curved teeth, serrated like kitchen knives, found their marks. And again. And again.

The turtle weighed close to 250 pounds. The shark was five times that, but the turtle would still have been enough to fill its stomach — if it weren't for the others. The tiger shark swam by itself for hundreds of miles, but when there was food, it was never alone.

As it circled around for another bite, a second shark flashed up from below. It was smaller and faster and just as hungry. It tore chunks of its own. And then another one appeared. With it came a cloud of the little scavenger fish that frustrated the big shark. They were too small and quick to catch, but big enough to snap up some of its kill.

The turtle was torn to pieces and devoured in a storm of blood.

3

Davey made it past the hotel's front desk — really a chest-high counter — without any trouble. Admittedly, there was no one there, so the only trouble would've been if he'd run into it. He didn't. He read the small RING FOR SERVICE! sign and he didn't do that, either. Then he pushed through the front door and stepped out into a truly gorgeous morning.

He could hardly believe it. In front of him, just past the hotel grounds, was a beach and then the ocean. The blue of the sky and the blue of the water met at the horizon. It was like another world, a fantasy realm.

He hadn't really seen the beach the day before. The coolest thing he'd seen then was the Cincinnati airport, where he'd been able to watch a few jets take off. It was too late to see much by the time they'd gotten to Florida. The taxi driver in Key West told them the sunset had been really great — and that they'd just missed it. The guy who piloted the little boat over to this island said the same thing. The boat ride was kind of cool, but there wasn't much to see in the dark. Davey's main impression of Florida so far had been of a nice thing he'd just missed.

He saw it all now, though. First up, a palm tree. Until that moment, palm trees had been one of those famous things he'd seen on TV but not in person. Palm trees, polar bears, riots . . . He stood there looking at it for a few seconds. It was just like on *Hawaii Five-0*. So far, he'd made it exactly four feet from the hotel.

He looked to the sides: more palms trees and a sandy walking path in both directions. He listened closely and could just hear the little waves curling and falling and retreating at the ocean's edge. He turned around and saw the sign on the front of the hotel. Swooping blue letters on a white background spelled out ASZURE ISLAND INN. *Two points off for spelling,* he thought, though he knew it was the same way on the map.

He picked a direction — left, just to be different — and started walking. It took him a few steps to register the temperature. Normally, he'd step out a door and right away his body would tell him that it was too hot or too cold. It was a lot of both back in Ohio. But this time, his body had no complaints. It was warm but not too hot. The light breeze was refreshing but not too cool. Davey knew it would probably heat up as the day went on, but he figured that would just make the breeze feel nicer.

So, yes, he was impressed. But then he spotted the flaw in the plan after a few more steps: There was nothing to do on this island.

Still in front of the hotel, he could already see the end of it. Not the end of the hotel; the end of the island. It was that small. He looked at the hotel again, just now realizing that it was the only one on the island. This was a one-horse town, and the hotel was that horse.

Wow, he thought, *Mom wasn't kidding.* The first time she'd told them about this trip, she'd described it as a "remote island retreat." Brando had groaned. Two of those words basically mean the same thing as *boring.* After that, she'd started calling it a "family retreat" to "recharge." You weren't allowed to groan at a "family" anything, and who didn't like to get charged? Anyway, it hadn't been up for a vote. They'd already purchased the tickets — some great deal online.

Davey kept walking, and then he saw something. It was some kind of stand, just off the path. *Hey now,* he thought. It was closed, but then it wasn't even seven in the morning. With the wooden shutters locked, it was impossible to tell what it sold, but it had to sell something. He squinted into the distance and saw another one. *Maybe there are some the other way, too,* he thought.

Davey didn't need much. At home, he spent most of his time in his room, and a lot of that reading. And he had his favorite books with him. His parents could recharge, and he could reread. A few weeks earlier he'd overheard his mom calling him "kind of monk-ish," but he didn't think she meant it entirely in a bad way. They had monks in their family, actual Tibetan monks. His parents' business sold arts and crafts from Tibet. Though if you wanted to know what most of the arguments were about, they didn't sell nearly as many as they used to.

It didn't take Davey long to reach the second stand. This one had metal shutters that were closed tight with big padlocks. There was a sign on top: ASZURE ISLAND BAR. Davey considered it. He'd been hoping for a place that sold comic books, or even regular ones. He knew that Ernest Hemingway used to live on Key West. He could see Key West from here, a fuzzy lump on the water. Davey hadn't read any of Hemingway's books yet, but he knew he wrote about bullfights and wars and other potentially interesting things. He flexed his left hand and felt the familiar weight of *The Silmarillion*.

A bar was okay, he decided. They'd have pretzels and potato chips and probably a few different kinds of soda. Plus, it would be fun to tell his parents, "Back in a minute, just going to the bar!"

Davey smiled for the first time in days. And then he heard something: voices, headed his way. He was at the far end of the island, where it came to a tip before bending back toward the other side of the hotel. That's where the voices were coming from. He'd had the whole island to himself until now, but not anymore. The voices were getting louder. Not wanting to go toward them, he looked around for an alternative.

Drew Dobkin wanted the world to know that she was being held here against her will. She'd wanted to go to Madrid or Miami or Mykonos. It didn't have to begin with an *M*; those were just examples. But it should have been somewhere with excitement and music and boys with tans to look at. She was fourteen now and needed to go on holiday somewhere appropriate. Well, she'd be fourteen in two months, but she was always one to round up.

But had she been asked? She had not! Her parents had simply found some great deal online and packed her up like so much luggage and shipped her here straight from England. Now they were stumbling around some little walking path with only a vague idea of what time it was. She checked her phone. No service, of course, but it worked as a watch. It was 12:28 in the afternoon back in Knutsford, and apparently 7:28 in the morning here. And what was this, anyway, a deserted island? Like the ones in the cartoons? They hadn't seen a single person since they'd left the hotel. And come to think of it, they hadn't seen anyone there, either.

"Lovely, though, isn't it?" said her mom, Kate.

Her dad, a man universally known as Big Tony, grunted in agreement. And then she got the distinct, annoying impression that they were waiting for her opinion on the matter. She flicked her eyes around a bit. She supposed it was quite pretty, in a boring sort of way. Instead of admitting it, she asked, "Can we go to Key West today?"

Her best friend, Becca, had told her that Key West was where the party was at. Her exact words: "Key West, that's where the party's at." Drew didn't need a full-on party, just some excitement and a bit of fun. Wasn't that what holidays were for? It made no sense to her to leave England to rest — England was already the sleepiest place on earth!

"Now hold on, then," said Big Tony, his first words of the day. "We just got here last night!"

"It speaks!" said her mom, acting astonished.

And then there they went, joking around and talking about anything other than Key West. Drew let them have their fun. She'd spotted something interesting up ahead. It was a little . . . what did you call it? A pier, or was it too small for that? A dock, maybe?

"Here's the boat place," she said. She pointed out over the water, a little farther up the path. There was a single boat tied up alongside.

"That the one we took last night?" said her mom. They headed off the path and toward the worn wooden dock. The boat was painted white and had the hotel's name on the back in blue, just above the blocky outboard motor.

"Don't think so," said her dad.

They crossed a little sliver of sand and stepped carefully onto the end of the dock. Drew expected it to shift and possibly sink, but it was sturdy enough. She looked down as she walked and could see the ocean sloshing underneath through the planks. She gave the weathered wood a closer look. "Pretty worn down, isn't it?" she said.

"Adds to the charm of the place, I'd imagine," said her mom.

"And the cost!" joked Big Tony.

"This must be where they bring the people over," said Kate, pointing to the side opposite the hotel launch. The wood seemed even more scratched up and worn out there, and there was a thick rope tied to the far post. It was just like the one securing the hotel boat, but this one was coiled up, waiting for the next arrival.

"Nice work, detective," said Big Tony.

Kate smiled. Drew flicked her eyes to the side and saw Key West, hazy in the distance. Then she smiled, too.

The family turned and headed back toward shore, with Drew last in line. At the end of the dock, they met someone. "Hello there, luv," said Kate to the little boy. "Where are you off to?"

The boy looked to be ten or eleven. He pointed out to sea, back toward Key West. Drew glanced at him. Technically, this was a boy with a tan, but definitely not what she'd meant.

"Well, that will be quite an adventure for you!" continued her mom.

The boy just nodded and took a seat on the edge of the dock.

"Little pirate, that one," said Big Tony as they resumed their trip along the walking path.

Drew took one last look over her shoulder and saw the boy's parents appear from the hotel grounds with their luggage. *They must be waiting for the first boat to show,* she thought. *There must be a schedule somewhere.*

"Dad?" she said.

"Yeah, luv?"

"How much was the boat last night?"

"One million pounds!" he said.

Her mom gave him a swat.

Her parents held hands and looked out at the water. Drew clasped her own hands together as a joke, but there was no one to appreciate her humor. She kicked at a seashell with her flip-flop. She was wearing a parentally approved combo of shorts and a light T-shirt. ("You can't just go walking around in your bathing suit all day," her mom had said. "You're English!") Even as early as it was here, she already felt the sun on her arms and legs. At least she'd get a tan. Those were hard to come by in Knutsford.

She looked out to sea, too, but it all sort of seemed the same to her. She tried the island side, and there, sitting up against the trunk of a palm tree, was another boy. This one looked older, almost her

16

age. He was somewhat tan, too, but she thought it might be the natural kind with him. He was in the shade and reading a book, after all.

He raised his head as she passed, but looked down quickly when he saw her.

Quiet as a church mouse, that one, she thought. *He'll be no fun at all.*

Her parents didn't even notice him. They'd just spotted the bar.

5

Davey stood up and brushed the sand from his butt. He was just going to have to move if there were going to be English people running all over the place. It was distracting. He'd heard enough to identify their accents and not much more. He had a pretty solid grasp of English accents from PBS.

This family didn't have the posh accents from *Downton Abbey* (his mom's favorite show). They sounded more like some of the characters on *Mystery!* (his dad's). And by some of the characters, he meant the criminals. And the guy who played Gimli the Dwarf in the Lord of the Rings movies. He didn't think they were really criminals, the way the parents held hands and joked around. And they definitely weren't dwarves.

The problem — the distraction — was their daughter. At least he assumed it was their daughter. Whatever branch of the family tree she fell off of, her T-shirt was so light that he could see her bathing suit right through it. Or, wait . . . was that *her bra*?

Yep, waaaaay too distracting. Their voices had faded away at this point, but he figured they'd be back. Or someone else would, probably wearing a tiny bikini or something else that would make it impossible for him to concentrate on reading his book. Plus, he was sitting, like, twenty yards from the bar stand. What if it opened up and he got drunk on the fumes? It seemed possible. He knew from science class that alcoholic solutions were prone to evaporation. He took a deep breath as he started walking back toward the pathway. The air did smell a little different. Was that the ocean or just a whole mess of rum? Man, he'd be in trouble then. Stumbling back into the hotel room completely blitzed on alcohol vapors.

He'd be in trouble anyway. He'd realized that right around the time he'd fully woken up, just outside the hotel door. One of his parents was going to wake up and see that he wasn't there. Then that one would wake up the other one so they could both have a mutual parental freak-out about it. He rehearsed possible excuses in his head:

"I was just sooo excited to get started on our awesome vacation!"

"I saw a beached whale from the window and went out to help."

"Brando was farting."

He didn't think any of those would cut it, so to speak. He tried to think of others, but the best he could come up with was: "Where was I going to go? It's a frickin' island!"

It was hopeless. He was thinking about that girl again. He wondered what her name was. Had they said it, in their criminal dwarfen accents? The only thing he remembered them calling her was "luv." And if he called her that, he'd straight up get smacked.

19

Luv . . . Now there's something he didn't hear in his family, not anymore. He picked at that thought for a bit until he saw the next family. They were sitting quietly on their luggage at the edge of a little dock, just off the walking path.

"Out for a walk?" called a very tall man.

Davey looked at him. The only thing louder than the man's voice was his shirt. A Hawaiian shirt in Florida . . . Those were some weak geographical skills right there.

"Yeah," Davey called back. He tried to think of something else to say so he could walk away from them without seeming rude. "Waiting for a boat?"

"Yeah," called the man. "First one of the day. We're not exactly sure when it's supposed to get here, but we've got an early flight."

That hadn't worked. Now he had to respond to that, too. He took another look at the little group. The lady was glancing over her shoulder and out to sea, as if mentioning the boat might've made it appear. There was a boy there, too, younger than Brando. The boy nodded at him, and Davey nodded back. He realized he still hadn't responded.

"Well, good luck with that!" he called. He gave a quick wave and started walking again before they could say anything else.

Once he was a safe distance away, he looked back. There was a white boat tied to the end of the dock. He sort of wanted to check it out. He also wanted to walk to the end of the dock and look into the deeper water. He bet there'd be fish and stuff. But he couldn't with all those people camped out at this end of it. What was it, rush hour all of a sudden? He kept walking, looking for a quiet spot to read his book.

The pathway connected to another one leading to the back of the hotel. There was a pool, which made no sense to him. The whole place was surrounded by ocean. He kept going and was all the way at the other end of the little island when he found it. A little path split off from the main one. He followed it through a thick stand of scrubby bushes and salt-stunted trees and emerged onto the most beautiful little beach he'd ever seen. The most beautiful, and the most private. There was absolutely no one there, and looking back, he could no longer see the walkway or the hotel or really much of anything.

In fact, the only evidence that anyone had *ever* been there before was a large sign, nearly falling over in the sand. The paint was sunblasted and peeling, but he could still make out most of the letters: NO SW MM NG.

He played a quick game of *Wheel of Fortune* in his head, bought a vowel: *No Swimming.*

6

Brando got up to go to the bathroom. He was so sleepy that he didn't notice his brother was gone until he got back. For a few moments he just stood at the end of his bed looking at the empty cot. At first he thought that something exciting might've happened. Maybe his brother had been carried off by a gator or captured by drug smugglers. He'd watched enough TV to know that Florida had both.

He walked over to the cot, knelt down, and looked underneath. Davey wasn't camped out under there. He looked over at his own bed: comfortable and warm. He could just go back to sleep and forget about it, but now he was curious. He knew his older brother well — he'd lived with him his entire life — so he knew what to look for.

He checked the floor on both sides of the cot, everywhere within an arm's length or so. Sure enough, Davey's glasses were gone. And where was that book he'd been carrying around all week, *The Silma-something-or-other*? He found Davey's little stack of books and checked each one. It was gone, too.

So he took his glasses and his book, thought Brando. *Probably his key card for the room, too.* That pretty much ruled out gator attack or kidnapping. Brando shrugged it off. That had been a long shot, anyway. So that meant . . .

Davey had snuck out of the room. It didn't surprise Brando that much. His brother was always wandering off to hang out by himself these days. He'd become so boring. But this was different. This wasn't heading straight up to his room after dinner. He could get in major trouble for this.

Brando reached down and felt the cot. The plan was for them to alternate nights on it. Their dad had called it an "army cot," trying to spin it into something cool. Brando wasn't fooled. He touched the metal frame and coarse canvas and could tell it would be seriously uncomfortable.

A plan took shape. If Davey got in trouble, he should have to sleep on the cot all week. That was only fair, right? Brando could just quietly suggest it at some point. He liked the plan, but now he was all kinds of conflicted. He was many things, most of which he'd admit with pride: loud, moody, maybe a little devious around the edges. But he was not a rat. And he had a lot of opinions about his older brother, who never wanted to hang out with him anymore. But he didn't hate him.

He looked back at his parents. He knew his dad was still asleep because he could hear him snoring, so he only really had to check on his mom. She was motionless, balanced on the very edge of the bed. How did she sleep through that noise at point-blank range? For a second Brando wondered if he snored, too. *Nah,* he thought. *Not me.*

He looked directly at them and thought, as hard as he could:

WAKE UP.

WAKE UP.

YOUR SON HAS FLOWN THE COOP — WAKE UP!

Nothing.

Brando made a deal with himself: He wouldn't intentionally wake them up. That would be the same as ratting on his brother. He'd just behave totally normally. If they happened to hear him and wake up before Davey got back, well, Davey had made his cot, and now he had to lie in it. All week.

Brando went over to the little desk, pulled out the chair, and sat down. He spent some time reading the room service menu. He considered his breakfast options. Then he got up and walked over to the mini fridge on the other side of the room. It was fairly close to his dad's head, but he wasn't especially careful opening it.

His dad didn't seem to notice. Brando pushed through all of the expensive stuff the hotel was trying to sell: the five-dollar pack of M&M's, the mixed nuts for seven fifty. He took out the half-full bottle of Coke he'd picked up in Key West and put in there last night. He undid the cap, but it was too flat to hiss or fizz or anything.

He wasn't supposed to have soda in the morning, but this was a no-lose situation for him. If his parents woke up right now, he wouldn't be the one in trouble. He stood right next to their bed and took a long drink. Still nothing. He put the cap back on and put it back in the mini fridge. He closed the door kind of hard. Wouldn't want to waste electricity.

His dad shifted in the bed. He started to roll over, but his body seemed to remember that it had nowhere to go and stopped. It amounted to a shoulder fake, one way and then the other. He even stopped snoring for a moment. Brando held his breath, but his dad went right back to snoring. His mom hadn't moved an inch.

Brando walked back across the room. He sat on the edge of his bed. It really was comfortable. He lay back to consider his next move. A minute later, he was snoring, too.

7

Davey was surprised how warm the water was. He was standing at the very edge of the breaking waves, up to his ankles. He'd kicked off his sneakers and walked right past the NO SW MM NG sign, which was fine because he wasn't sw mm ng. He still had his glasses on, still had the book in his hand. He was just testing out the water for later.

He figured he'd go in that afternoon — if he wasn't hotel-grounded, anyway. That would be fine with him, too. That was Davey's secret weapon. Most of the things his parents could do to punish him — send him to his room, revoke TV privileges — he did to himself anyway. If they really wanted to get to him, they could take his books away. That might work, but no parent ever did that. In parent logic, that would be like forbidding him from doing his homework.

The little waves curled around his ankles, clean and clear and warm. They seemed almost friendly. It was like being licked by a giant kitten, he thought — except not as weird or creepy as that. He looked out over the water and could see all the way to the horizon. He felt like an explorer. There was nothing in between him and the edge of the world. He remembered the sight of Key West off in the distance from the other side of the island. He pictured the image of Aszure Island he'd seen on Google Maps. If Key West was east of here, then he was looking at the open ocean to the west now. Next stop: Mexico, a thousand miles away.

A larger wave broke in front of him, sending water halfway up his shin. He reached down and ran his right hand through it as it rushed past, clutching his book to his chest with his left. It was like a bath, like stepping into a vast, gently rolling bath. The water tugged at his calves as it rushed back out to sea, and he stood up to steady himself.

Maybe this week won't be so bad, after all, he thought as he walked out of the water and back up the beach. If he stood right in the breakers the whole time, he'd hardly be able to hear his family. Or maybe if he just didn't tell them about this little spot . . . He looked around the little beach. He had it to himself and could sit anywhere. He chose a spot at the edge of the trees, where he could be half in and half out of the sun.

He sat down, opened his book to the page he'd dog-eared, and got started. He read for a while, but he wasn't quite as lost in it as he had been the first two times he'd read it. He kept looking up at the sea. He watched the little waves build themselves up and fall over. He watched the foamy white breakers that had pushed and pulled playfully at his ankles.

He decided to go in again, maybe just a little farther this time.

He hadn't put his sneakers back on, so he didn't have to worry about them. Sand clung unevenly to his feet like threadbare socks. He took the key card and the eight dollars — a five and three ones, folded neatly — out of the pocket of his swim trunks. He looked around to make sure there were no witnesses and took his T-shirt off. He figured he'd go in up to his waist.

He looked down at his little pile of stuff and then looked over at the mouth of the path. No one else had come through it so far, but it was just a couple dozen yards from the main walkway. Better safe than sorry. He bundled up all his stuff, sneakers included, and walked back to the line of trees. He found a bush that was a little greener and less patchy than the others and stashed his stuff underneath the far side. He got a nasty scratch on his arm from one of the sharp little branches. It turned red with tiny pinpricks of blood as he walked across the sand. It didn't bother him. He used to get a lot of cuts and scratches back when he and his brother used to roam around the neighborhood, climbing trees and crashing through bushes. When he turned around, he couldn't see his stuff at all. He was satisfied, except . . .

He reached up and took off his glasses. Just in case. He'd only had them for a year. He'd gotten them when he'd started having trouble seeing what his teachers were writing on the board. He jogged over and put them under the bush as well, careful not to scratch himself this time. He kicked the sand around as he walked back so there wouldn't be an obvious line of footprints heading right toward his eight bucks. He stopped after a while. The sand was too fine to hold a shape for long.

He passed that sign again. *Relax, little sign,* he thought. *Don't lose any more letters worrying about me. I'm just going to wade around for a few minutes.* The sign was probably just there because there was no lifeguard on duty or something dumb like that anyway.

He marched right into the water this time. He didn't even pause at the line of breakers. It was so great because he didn't have to hold his breath for that first shock of cold, the way he did at the lake back home. He didn't have to go slowly, waiting for his body to adjust. He just strode forward like a hero heading into battle.

He braced himself for the force of the first wave. It hit him at the knees and splashed up the front of his trunks. The waves were bigger now. The tide was coming in.

8

Drew was on the roof of the hotel. She'd found the sun deck. It was still too early for proper sunbathing, she supposed, but it was a nice opportunity to give her parents the slip. They were in the lobby waiting — dead serious — for the gift shop to open. As if they didn't have all week. Plus, she could give her bikini a test run before they all headed to the beach later.

She was standing at the railing and looking out over the little island. She could see nearly all of it from up here. "I am the master of all I survey," she told herself, "the queen of my castle." But then she gazed out over the water and saw the hazy lump of Key West, and she knew the truth. A queen, maybe, but in exile.

She lowered her gaze and saw the dock again. She tried to find the little boy from earlier, but it was impossible. He was just one small figure among many now. There were other kids, and other parents, too. A small crowd had gathered, still waiting for the first boat of the day.

A pile of luggage was growing at the edge of the dock. Drew looked at the pile, looked at the people, looked back at the pile, added it up. It wasn't enough luggage for the number of people. That meant some of them were just going into Key West for the day. She heard her friend's voice: "where the party's at." She needed to figure out how to get on that boat.

Her parents would never let her go alone. She had to give up on that dream right now. They simply wouldn't. And if she snuck off and hopped on the boat right before it left, they'd hop right on the next one. They'd comb every square centimeter of the place until they found her, shouting "Drew-Bear! Drew-Bear!" the whole time and embarrassing her to high heaven.

No, she'd have to bring them, and even that wouldn't be easy. She'd have to work on them, convince them. She made up her mind to start later that day. A few casual comments here and there, just to plant the seed.

She wandered over to the railing and looked out into the distance. It was open ocean as far as the eye could see: clear blue tropical water, shadow and light and wind playing over its surface. Her mom was right; it was quite pretty.

She took one last look over toward Key West as she tugged her shorts up her legs, and there it was, a fat boat making slow progress across the water. The little crowd was more animated now, as if someone had stepped on their anthill. She pulled her shirt over her head, found her second flip-flop, and headed down to find her parents. The restaurant would be open now, and she was hungry.

*   *   *

Down at the dock, the fat-bottomed boat bumped to a stop against the rubber tires strung along the side of the pilings. The day manager of the hotel was there to meet it and throw the rope.

"Hey, Zeke," he said to the boat's captain.

"Hey, Marco," said the captain.

Zeke's real name was Jonathan Palpen, but he'd learned long ago that the tourists preferred something a little more down-home. He'd picked Zeke off a show about gator wrestlers.

"Hold on now, folks," Zeke called. The tourists on board were already standing up and trying to get off the boat. The ones onshore were already rumbling down the dock, jockeying for position. Sundays were always the worst. "Let me tie up first!"

There was a little edge in his voice that made them listen. Zeke had been out at the local bars the night before. It was what they called "a late night" in most places, but in Key West they just called it Saturday. He tied up, fore and aft, and then squinted up into the sunlight. He eyeballed the count: maybe a dozen, most with luggage. It would be close to capacity.

"Let 'em off first," he called, as the inbound passengers began to file off the boat. He didn't bother to soften his voice. The tourists liked that, too. Captain Zeke, with his tattered white captain's hat, short temper, and faint smell of booze — so authentic!

"Marco, my man, can you help me collect the money?" he called, even louder. "Five bucks a head, no exceptions!"

"Sure thing, Zeke!" called Marco.

They always did it this way because some of the outgoing guests would give Marco one last tip, a few dollar bills to go along with the fiver for the boat. Marco would then quietly slip some of the haul over to Zeke, along with the outgoing mail and any FedEx packages that needed to be dropped in the box at the marina.

The tourists bumped and jostled their way along the dock, out of and into the boat. Luggage was dropped from the boat onto the dock and vice versa. And all that sound was conducted into the water, through the wood of the dock or the bottom of the boat. It was a thick bass beat, an irregular, spastic drumming, an entire rhythm section of commerce.

It carried through the water, and it didn't go unnoticed. Some days, Zeke would see a small shark come right alongside the boat to investigate, maybe a spinner or even a blue. Some days he saw something larger. Today, he mostly just saw luggage. He eyed the tags as he stowed the cases: *EYW* for the little airport on Key West, *FLL* or *MIA* for the larger ones in Fort Lauderdale or Miami. That last one always seemed unlucky to him: *MIA* . . . missing in action. Maybe that's why he never made it up that far.

Some of the passengers greeted him. They remembered him from the trip out or the year before, or even the day before for the day-trippers. He grunted a response. The truth was they all sort of blended together after a while, different faces every day of every week of every year.

Soon the money had been collected and the luggage stowed. The ropes that had just been thrown on were thrown off. Marco gave them a theatrical wave. "Thanks again for choosing the Aszure Island Inn!" he called as the old boat began to putter away. "Tell your friends!"

The passengers waved back at him and then turned around to face forward. Most of them had long trips ahead, long trips to cold places. Zeke kept his eyes on the water ahead. A long, dark shadow crossed paths with the boat sixty yards out and slipped silently underneath. A part of the creature's primitive brain told it to follow this noisy thing. It knew what it was now. But it was too small. It was the big ones that sometimes left food in their wakes. It was the ones as big as a dozen whales that were worth following. Not this one.

The shark glided silently on.

9

Davey was in up to his waist. That's as far as he'd planned to go, but the breakers were coming in right at stomach height and really letting him have it. He decided to wade out a little farther, just past them. It's not like he would get any wetter. The waves had already declared a splash fight and won handily. When Davey pushed his hand back through his hair, he was surprised to find it slick as an otter's. He didn't care; he was having fun. He waded out a little farther.

He'd just been through an entire Ohio winter: bleak and gray and cold. He'd spent almost all of it inside, and most of that in his room. This felt good. Splashing around in the sun. The water gave him a little tug under the surface, and he let out a little bark of laughter as he regained his balance. The splash fight was over, and the sea had just challenged him to a game of tug-of-war.

He wasn't even sure which sea. His best guess was the Gulf of Mexico, but there was a chance it was the Caribbean. He made a mental note to check when he got back to the hotel room. As soon as he thought about that dark, crowded, smelly little room, he knew he'd made the right decision. Whichever sea it was, even if it was still just the Plain-Jane Atlantic, everyone back at school would be impressed.

He walked parallel to shore for a while. He looked back at the beach. It looked smaller than he remembered, and he had no trouble taking it all in. He was still alone. He saw the sign leaning over in the sand. He couldn't read it from here without his glasses, but he knew what it said. He thought about swimming a little anyway. Just a few strokes to say he did it. He was a pretty good swimmer. He and Brando used to go down to the lake every day, back when he did things like that.

The ocean had gone quiet around him. He was so lost in thought that it took him a while to notice. When he did, he looked out to sea. The surface was flat in front of him. He assumed it was because he was out past the surf line. But when he looked in toward shore, the surface was flat there, too.

It was the strangest thing. There were breakers on both sides of it, and then this band of flat water in between. It was as if something was knocking the waves down here. And something else seemed weird. It was the breakers; they'd moved so far in toward shore.

He got a sick feeling in his gut.

He took a breath and told himself not to panic.

The breakers hadn't moved farther in. He'd gone farther out. Much farther than he'd intended. Much, much farther. The water was up to the middle of his chest, and suddenly that seemed way too deep.

He stopped walking and felt the same tug under the surface that he'd felt before. And now the panic flooded through him: It had never stopped. He'd been walking against it this whole time. It had pulled him a little farther out with each step, leading him along like a bad friend. He looked down. The water was so clear that he could see his feet. He could practically count his toes. But he was so far from shore. The slope had been gentle up to this point, but it could drop off five, ten, twenty feet at any moment. He'd be in over his head — over his head in some sea he couldn't even name.

He started in toward shore. At least he tried to. He took a big step, and then another. He pushed his legs through the water as hard as he could. But the water pulled back just as hard. Every time his feet left the bottom, the sea tugged him backward. After half a dozen steps, he was sure he was no closer to shore.

His forehead was still slick with water, but he felt the sweat break out along it in little pinpricks. He decided to swim for it. He lunged forward and began kicking before his face even hit the water. Once it did, he began throwing his arms forward.

His fear wanted him to flail away, to scratch and claw at the surface. He didn't let himself. He needed to do this right. He remembered his lessons, maintained proper form. He kicked with his legs and pulled his outstretched hands through the water in full, even strokes. He looked to the side to get his air.

And he needed that air. His lungs began to burn almost immediately. It had been a long time since he'd swum to anything farther out than the raft at the lake. And even that was a while ago. He'd barely gone to the lake at all the summer before. He remembered the swim in from the year before that. How he would run the length of the raft and dive headfirst. He'd glide and kick to see how far he could go underwater. By the time he'd come up, he'd be halfway to shore.

The memory was so strong that Davey expected to be halfway to the beach by now. He was tired and needed a break anyway, so he broke his rhythm and took a quick look forward. If he'd had enough air in his lungs, he would've screamed. The beach was farther away now. It looked so small, like he could hold it in his hand. So small, and so empty. He wanted to call for help, but there was no one there.

It had been a mistake to swim. He knew that now. He stopped kicking and let his feet fall back underneath him. He pushed his arms sideways through the water to keep his head and shoulders steady. In a few moments, he was straight up and down in the water. But he wasn't standing. His feet could no longer reach the bottom.

He kicked a few times, just to stay afloat. He took a few quick gulps of air. And then he began kicking and throwing his arms forward. He scratched at the surface of the water. He clawed.

10

Panic turned to desperation and Davey turned that into effort. He was cranking out more effort than he ever had. Swimming had been a mistake — this whole thing had been a mistake! But here he was, and swimming was all he had now. He just needed to try harder, to get back to where his feet could touch.

But desperation is a fast-burning fuel. His muscles ached as he threw them forward. His lungs screamed for more oxygen. His rhythm fell apart. He turned his head to the side to breathe, but he got greedy. He was still sucking in air as his head turned back down. He inhaled bitter salt water and coughed facedown in the sea. More water slipped in. He spit out as much as he could and kept going.

He was no quitter. He never had been. He could read an entire book in one sitting. A lot of people have probably done that, but for Davey, the book might be four hundred pages and the sitting six hours. He'd won races in gym by being kind of fast for longer than his classmates could be really fast. And Davey was pretty sure that if he stopped trying now, he would die. Keep trying or die. It wasn't even a question.

As he got farther from shore, he approached a sandbar lurking under the surface. That's what had caused this. As the ocean had pushed forward and the waves had piled onto shore, tremendous pressure had built up for all that water to get back out to sea. The sandbar had shifted, as it did sometimes, and a gap had opened up. The water had found the gap and rushed back through it. People called them riptides, but they weren't really tides at all. Rip current was more accurate. That's what they were: currents, shifting and dangerous.

Davey had started counting his strokes in sets of four. It helped calm his raging mind and gave him something to focus on. He couldn't keep swimming forever, but he could do another four. On the fourth stroke of his next set, he forced himself a little farther up out of the water. He sucked in a lungful of much-needed oxygen and risked a quick look forward. With water in his eyes and without his glasses, the beach was a blur of color far away. Still so far away. He fell back into the water. Higher up meant deeper down, and now he was under the surface.

It was quiet under here. Even his aching muscles eased a bit in the warm churn. It was almost peaceful. *This is how I'll die,* he thought. *Under the warm, clear water.* They say that, right before death, your whole life flashes in front of you in seconds. And if a whole life takes seconds for an adult, how long does it take for a thirteen-year-old? And how long does just one memory take? It flashed into Davey's mind fully formed, like a fish pulled from the water.

It was his family's last vacation, two years ago. They'd skipped last year. They were staying with relatives in Colorado and had spent a day riding down a fast-moving river on inner tubes. They were all bundled in fancy, neon-yellow life jackets. Fallen tree branches had snagged on the river bottom and collected into big bird-nest-looking tangles in some places.

The family had sailed past the first few with their dad calling out orders: "Watch out!" and "Left, left, left!" or "Right, right, right!" But Brando had managed to bull's-eye the third one. He rode the fast-moving current right into the center of it, and his tube stuck fast. Brando popped right out of it and into the water. His life jacket had been way too big for him, and he'd bobbed down the river like a yellow rubber ducky. Their mom angled over and scooped him up. No harm, no foul, except that now his tube was hung up on branches back upstream.

They'd left a security deposit, and their dad was determined to get the tube back. The rest of them angled their tubes over into the shallow water along the bank and watched. He took off his life jacket, dove into the water, and swam for it.

Tam was a good swimmer. At first, he made some progress. It was two steps forward with every powerful stoke. But the current would push him one step back on every little pause in between. He made it maybe ten feet back upriver before the ratio started to reverse. One step forward with every stroke, two steps back with every pause. Pretty soon he was right back where he started. He'd looked at his family, surprised to see them right there. Davey remembered his father's face, exhausted and embarrassed.

Tam had dived back in. Tried again. But this time he hadn't even made it five feet, not even the length of his body. In the end, he had to walk through the bushes and prickers along the bank, wearing just his shorts and life jacket. He got scratched and cut and stung by a bee. He got upstream of the tube, dove back in, and got a hold of it, but he never said another thing about it.

Davey pushed back to the surface. His muscles roared with outrage. They thought they were done with effort, done with everything. But he battled on. He breathed in quick gulps, but water still slipped in, this time through his nose. He cleared it as best he could, but he could feel himself beginning to hyperventilate. He pushed his muscles to the point of exhaustion and then past that.

All that effort, and this time he was the one who couldn't make it five feet. A river in the sea. That was the only way he could understand it: He was in a river in the sea. How could he fight a thing like that? How could he win when even his dad had given up?

He gave up and the current took him. The sun pushed light through his closed eyelids. He was barely conscious, floating backward. Some primitive part of his brain — not even human, really — kept his systems going. The rest of his brain — all the higher functions, the brain that had been able to read a fat book in one sitting — could hold only one simple thought now: *Stay afloat.* His legs twitched when they could into something like a kick. *If you can, stay afloat.*

And he was carried out to sea.

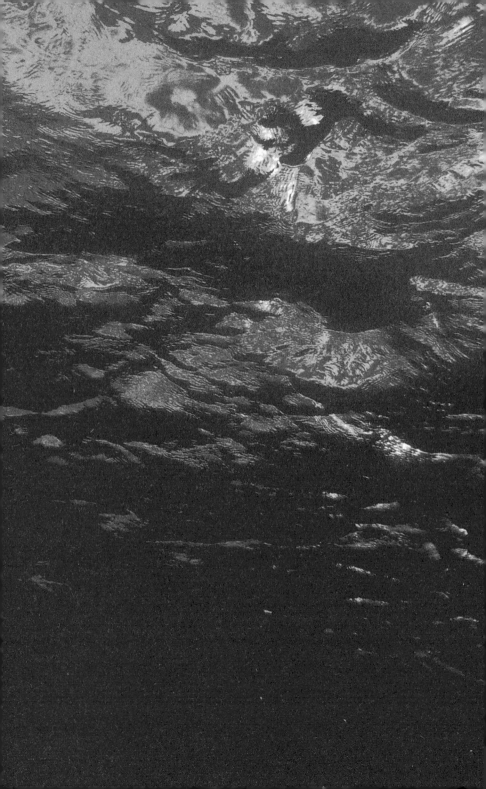

PART TWO

BOY AND SEA

11

Brando fell off the bed. It was bound to happen. He'd fallen asleep on the very edge of the thing. He rolled one way to get more comfortable. Then he rolled back and onto the floor. His head pumpkin-thunked on the soft carpet.

"Corn dog!" he blurted. It's what he said when his Spider-Sense told him his parents were around.

They'd been close to waking anyway. Now, as if they were garage doors activated by the words *corn dog*, they rose. His mom sat straight up in bed like a zombie rising from an autopsy table. His dad finally stopped snoring. In the sudden quiet, Brando could hear him throw off the covers on the far side of the bed.

Pamela was the first to speak. "Brando?" she said. "Davey? Was that you?"

From her perch on the bed, she could see neither of her sons.

Brando rubbed his head and heard himself say, "Davey's not here."

And, oh boy, that did it. Pamela followed his voice down. She wasn't especially surprised to find her youngest on the floor in between the beds. Then she looked over at the cot and her mouth dropped open.

"What do you mean, 'not here'?" she said at the exact same moment that Tam said, "Well, where is he?"

Brando got to his feet. His mom's face was puffy from sleep. The side of his dad's face was a web of red lines from where it had been pressing against the pillow. Brando almost felt bad for them. They'd been awake for seconds on the first day of their first vacation in two years and they already had something to be mad about. He was just glad it wasn't him. "How should I know?" he said.

Three minutes later, they were at the front desk. Marco, long back from the dock, was on the other side.

"Has our son been past here?" said Tam.

Uh-oh, thought Marco, but what he said was: "What does your son look like?"

Tam waved his hand toward Brando. "Like this one, but a little bigger," he said. "Has glasses."

Marco looked at Brando and tried to picture him older and with glasses. "Sorry," he said. "Not this morning."

"How long have you been back there?" said Pamela, still tugging at the sundress she'd thrown on.

"Do you mean behind the desk?" said Marco. For some reason, he didn't like the phrase *back there.*

"Yes," she said. "Obviously."

Marco didn't like that *obviously*, either, but he took a deep breath and told her, "About half an hour."

"That's not very long," said Pamela.

Marco did not like this lady.

"Who was here before you?" said Tam, trying to edge back into the conversation.

Marco knew this would set the lady off, but he said it anyway. "No one. It's ring for service during overnight hours."

"What? That's . . . I've never even . . ." sputtered Pamela before collecting herself. "I've never been to a hotel that didn't have *someone* on duty!"

Marco wanted to say, *Well, you've probably never been to a hotel on a tiny island before. We don't get a lot of walk-in business from frickin' dolphins!* Instead, another deep breath. "Well," he said, "I can tell you that he didn't ring the bell."

Pamela glared at him, but Tam pulled her away. "Thank you very much," he said. "I'm sure he's just checking things out."

Marco nodded and gave them a halfhearted smile.

Brando followed his parents toward the front door. He was close enough to hear his dad whisper to his mom, "Don't make him mad. We might need his help this week."

"I hope not," she whispered.

They pushed through the glass double doors and began calling out Davey's name. Brando trailed after them, mortified.

"Davey!" shouted Tam. His voice was blunt and loud.

"Davey!" called Pamela, her voice sharper and still a little raspy.

Brando kept his mouth shut. An older couple out for a walk turned and stared at them, and Brando burned with embarrassment. *Yep,* he thought, *the Tserings have arrived.*

His parents looked around and stopped shouting. They could see the whole front of the hotel and most of the main beach from here, and the old couple were the only people in sight.

"Least he won't get lost in the crowd," said Tam.

"We should've gotten coffee first," said Pamela, batting his arm.

That's when Brando realized that they weren't all that concerned. And why should they be? It was an island. How far could Davey go? They weren't even especially mad. Brando exhaled. *Good,* he thought. *Maybe they won't kill him when they find him.*

"Maybe there's somewhere out here that sells it," said Tam. "I think I see some kind of stand up the path."

He pointed to the left. Pamela leaned over to look around him. Two sharp thumps carried through the air as the stall's storm shutters were thrown open. "Looks like they're opening up."

Without another word, they began walking in that direction. Adults and their coffee. Brando didn't understand it: The stuff tasted like motor oil. But he knew that they were now looking for two things: one was served in a cup, the other wore glasses.

He looked around as they walked. It was seriously nice out here, and it felt good to be outside without a jacket. He looked up at his parents. They were looking around, too. He followed his mom's eyes out to sea and saw that she had the beginnings of a smile on her face. That was good for her, especially these days. He was now ready to contribute to the search.

"He took his book," he said.

"What's that?" said Tam.

"He took that book. It wasn't with the others."

His parents were quiet for a few moments, and then Tam broke the silence. "Ha!" he barked.

Pamela smiled, a real smile this time. "Our outlaw son," she said. "Sneaking off to read."

They both laughed. They didn't look at each other when they did, but they still kind of shared a laugh. Brando hadn't seen them do that in a long time, and it made him feel good.

"Keep an eye out for the reflection off his glasses!" he said, and got a few more little laughs out of them. They were making the most of it, but the mood started to change after that. The farther they went with no sign of Davey, the tenser they got.

"I was sure he'd be right outside," said Tam.

"On one of those chairs out front or maybe that little patio," said Pamela, picking up the thought.

Their heads were on a swivel now. Their lazy looks to the side had become sharp turns toward the slightest sound. They began stepping off the walkway to look behind trees or down side paths.

And then they began calling out again. His mom stuck with his name, just "Davey! Davey!" over and over. His dad mixed it up sometimes with a "Where are you, champ?"

It didn't bother Brando as much anymore. He wasn't too worried. Davey had been going places without his parents — the lake, the store, the library — since he was nine or ten. And not just going to those places, but taking Brando there, too. So he wasn't exactly worried. Not exactly. But he wasn't embarrassed by the calls anymore, either.

He saw a woman walking along the edge of the beach with a baby slung to her front in a harness. He pointed her out, and his mom walked over and did the talking. "Have you seen a young boy? About this tall? With glasses?"

Even from back on the walkway, Brando could see that she was embarrassed. She'd lost her boy, and here this woman was holding her child closer than her purse. His mom didn't like being embarrassed at all. She wouldn't do it if she wasn't at least a little worried.

The stand they'd seen opening up did sell coffee, but the first batch wasn't quite ready when they got there.

"Five minutes," said the man, who hadn't seen Davey, either.

They could already smell it beginning to brew, but they didn't wait.

12

Davey opened his eyes to a nightmare. Ocean. Ocean forever. He tried to figure out how long he'd drifted and how far he might have gone. But his memories were vague and dreamlike. He remembered floating on his back when he could and treading water when he had to. He remembered flickering on the edge of consciousness, slipping under the surface, pushing his way back.

He didn't know how far he'd gone or even in which direction. All he knew for sure was that the current had finally let go of him, and he was very far from land. He straightened himself up in the water. His legs felt rubbery and numb as they churned slowly underneath him. They moved just enough to keep his mouth above the water. When he needed to, he flapped his arms to help. They hurt more, weren't as numb. He wasn't sure if that was good or bad.

Little waves pushed him around, and fear punched him in the gut. He was out here alone, in deep water. Anything could be in here with him. It could be just below him, or just behind. *Sharks.* The word popped into his head. He looked down into the clear blue depths. Under the surface, his legs somehow looked both short and far away. At the end of them, he saw his feet, moving slowly back and forth. He saw no other shapes. But there was another fear lurking inside him, this one as big as the entire ocean. He tried not to give it a name, but it already had one. *Drowning.*

He squinted into the distance. He looked at the horizon the way he used to look at the board before he got his glasses. *His glasses.* The thought gutted him. How was he supposed to see land when he couldn't tell the difference between an *E* and a *Z* from twenty feet away? Still, he had to try. His arms, his legs — they wouldn't last much longer out here. The small swells were making him work harder, sapping what was left of his energy.

He pushed his arms clockwise through the water and kicked a little harder with his right leg. Slowly, he began to turn. He squinted into the distance as he went. *Please, please, please,* he thought.

Nothing this way.

Nothing that way.

Nothing that way, either.

And then, when he was sure he must have gone all the way around already, he saw it. Had it been there before? Had he missed it? It wasn't much, just a hazy blue-gray lump off in the distance. *Thank God,* he thought. *Thank God.* He didn't know if it was the island he'd come from or a different island. And he didn't care. It could have been the Island of Boy-Eating Monsters and he would've been thrilled.

He stopped squinting. It got a little fuzzier. But now that he knew where to look, he could still see it. The next question, the big one: Could he reach it? The thought of swimming filled him with a profound and heavy tiredness. He felt like he'd already swum enough for a lifetime today.

He couldn't let himself think about it. If he didn't swim now, he wouldn't get another chance. It really *would* be enough for a lifetime. He lowered his head. He told his legs to kick, told his arm to rise up and fall forward. He didn't know if any of that would happen until it did.

Slowly, and just barely, he began to swim. It seemed so crazy to him because he was pretty sure he was heading right back in the direction he'd just come from. Why did he expect this time to be any different?

He pushed the thought out of his mind. He tried to replace it with something better. He thought about what he'd do when he got back to land. First, he'd just lie on whatever beach he washed up on for a very long time. Maybe a day. Then he'd get up and walk or crawl or roll or whatever he could manage until he found his parents. He pictured his mom and dad, and the first thing he thought was, *I'm in trouble. They're going to be so mad.* A second later, that seemed funny to him. *In trouble? Ya think?* Facedown in the water, just for a second, he smiled.

And then he thought, *I'm definitely getting that bed tonight. Brando can have the cot, and he'd better not say anything about it, either. I'm a year and a half older, and that's that.*

He looked up to make sure he was still headed in the right direction, and he was surprised to see how much bigger the island looked already. It seemed like a weird shape for an island, but then he'd never seen one from out on the water before. He dropped his head down and kept going.

The burning ache was returning to his muscles now. It wasn't as bad as before yet, but it wasn't good, either. How many strokes did he have left in his arms? he wondered. How many kicks did he have left in his legs? Would it be enough?

He stopped thinking about it, and for a while he just swam. He made slow, uneven progress. He wouldn't have been surprised if jellyfish were passing him. But at least he was headed in the right direction. At least he was making progress. He might even make it.

He made himself wait before he looked up at the island again. It was a waste of energy, and it threw his rhythm off. But it was the only thing that kept him going. He made another deal with himself: Four more good strokes and he could take a quick look. He wanted to see how big it looked now. He wanted to know that he was getting closer to his destination.

And he was. He was getting so much closer, in fact, that on the third stroke, he hit the island with his head. It made a hollow plastic *BONK* that he could hear right through the water.

13

The second stand was a lot like the first. It was about the size of a toolshed back in Ohio, but made of weathered wood with no-nonsense metal storm shutters on the front. The big difference was that the shutters were still closed on this one.

"No coffee here, either," said Tam. He looked back down the walkway. The coffee would be ready back at that first stand by now.

Pamela pointed to the sign on top: ASZURE ISLAND BAR. "Might have Irish coffee," she said.

"*Mom,*" said Brando. He was twelve, and he already knew you weren't supposed to make jokes about the Irish drinking.

"That's what it's called," she said.

"Really?" He filed the information away. Irish coffee: a joke you were allowed to make because it was true.

The stand faced out onto a beach, which more or less faced a bigger island off in the distance. "What's that?" asked Brando, pointing to it.

"Key West," said Tam.

"Bet this beach is popular," said his mom, nodding in front of them.

Brando looked around. "There's no one on it now," he said.

She smiled. It was a small, not particularly happy smile. "The bar's not open yet," she said.

They were moving on when they heard something from inside the stand. It was a loud thump followed by a sharp voice. That meant the same thing in Florida as it did in Ohio: Someone had just dropped something.

Tam ducked his head around the far side of the stand. Sure enough, there was a door there, and it was slightly open. He looked over at Pamela, and she nodded. He walked toward the door, and Brando followed a few steps behind. He'd never seen the inside of a bar before.

Brando could hear more sounds inside as they approached: footsteps, shuffling. Someone was moving stuff around in there. He watched his dad knock. The sounds stopped. Whoever was inside was playing dead. Brando had done the same thing himself when people came to the door, muting the TV, lying low. Davey basically did it all the time now, up in his room. He nodded toward his dad: *Don't be fooled.*

Tam knocked again, and the guy gave up. More shuffling, and then the door swung outward. Tam stepped back quickly, narrowly avoiding getting door-punched. A man ducked his head out and said, "Come back at eleven. Mimosas and Bloody Marys. Full bar at noon."

He began to close the door. Brando couldn't help but stare at his head. He had silver-gray hair, which Brando had seen plenty of times before. But his skin was something else entirely. It was tanned now and had probably been tanned steadily for the last five or six decades. Which is to say, it was something like leather. Brando smiled. *Davey would love this old dude. He's just like the characters in his books.*

"Wait," said Tam, and he grabbed the door.

Already staring at the man's face, Brando could see he wasn't happy about it. The man looked at Tam's hand. Then he ducked his head out a little farther and looked at Tam's face. "Like I said," he snapped. "Can't serve you till eleven!"

"We're not looking for drinks," said Tam. His voice wasn't hard or angry, but it wasn't soft, either. "We're looking for a boy."

The man seemed confused for a second. He had the look of someone who hadn't gotten much sleep. To Brando, he looked kind of like a tired wallet. "We don't sell those, either," said the man. "Maybe in Miami."

He looked over and caught Brando staring.

"You already got one, anyhow," he added. He still didn't look happy, but he'd stopped trying to pull the door closed.

"No, another one, our other son," said Tam.

"It's just that he's . . . Well, he's wandered off," said Pamela.

Brando and the man were equally surprised. Neither one had seen her walk over from the path.

The man's grim expression softened some. Maybe it was because

61

he'd figured out what was going on or maybe it was because the mother of the boy was present. "Well, I'm sorry, ma'am," he said, "but I ain't seen no boy around this morning. 'Cept this one here." He nodded toward Brando. Brando nodded back.

Tam's hand fell from the door. The man searched his morning-clouded mind for something encouraging to end on.

"Small island; you'll find 'im," he said. Then he tugged the door shut behind him.

Tam immediately knocked again.

"I'll keep an eye out!" the man called from inside, and that was the end of that.

They continued down the walkway, turned the corner, and headed down the other side of the island. *So far, it's shaped like an eye,* thought Brando.

Very quickly, they came across the dock. There were already a few people gathering for the next boat. They headed off the path to go ask them the same question they'd asked everyone else.

"We should print out a picture," said Pamela. "We could just show it to them."

The thought really bothered Brando, but he couldn't say exactly why.

"Let's at least go all the way around the island first," said Tam. Brando could tell from his voice that the idea bothered him, too. "We're not even halfway."

"I think we are," said Pamela under her breath.

Brando looked over just in time to see their flat expressions blossom into big fake smiles for the people at the start of the dock. And that really bothered him.

"Hello there!" called Tam. Pamela chipped in with a friendly wave.

Brando watched as a man stepped forward to greet his dad. They were about the same age and height. For some reason, they shook hands.

"What's all the excitement here?" said his dad.

"Waiting for the boat back, unfortunately," said the other man, as if he was trying to sell them a car. "Our time is up. Great week!"

"There's a boat this early?" said Tam.

"Oh, sure," said the other man. "Think this is the second one. Should be here any minute. Busy day at the checkout desk."

A family of four joined the group as he was talking, proving his point nicely.

"Well, I won't keep you," said Tam. "The thing is — craziest thing — our oldest son seems to have . . ."

Brando didn't listen to the rest. Behind him, his mom was already asking the new family the same thing. Instead, he walked out onto the dock.

"Don't fall in, sport!" called his dad.

"Be careful!" called his mom.

Their voices were a little too eager, their calls directed more toward the small crowd than their son. The message: *We are not bad parents!*

Yeah, yeah, thought Brando, holding up his hand. He was looking at the boats. There was the white hotel launch, which looked new and sleek and cool. And there was another boat tied up next to it now.

It was an old motorboat. Everything about it was battered. The paint was largely gone and the engine looked primitive, like the first one ever invented. Looking at it, Brando thought there was a small chance it was powered by steam. Even empty and tied to the dock, the boat listed alarmingly to one side. All of which made this boat, of course, much, much cooler.

Brando knew immediately that it belonged to the weather-beaten old man at the bar stand. It was like the boat version of that guy. He looked back over his shoulder. His mom and dad were done working the crowd. They waved at him to come back. From the looks on their faces, he knew that they hadn't gotten any information.

He had a new idea. He'd ditch them, too. He'd ditch them and spend the whole week hanging out with the old guy. He'd ride in the dangerous boat at top speed and listen to stories. Not the kind of stories that Davey liked, but real ones. Stories about people who drank Irish coffees, people who weren't even necessarily Irish.

He thought about it some more as he rejoined his parents on the shore. When they left all the people behind and continued down the walkway, he wondered where they were all going. For a few moments, he thought about both things at once. He thought about anything, in short, other than the fact that his brother was still missing. He thought about anything other than the fact that he had known before anyone and had done nothing about it. He already knew that.

14

Davey recoiled the way you do when something hits you in the head. Think dodgeball. The difference being that he was in deep water, in every sense. He stopped his legs midkick. He flapped his arms under the water — once, twice, three times. His head moved backward above the water as his feet continued to drift slowly forward underneath it.

The thing floated in the water in front of him. It was still bobbing lazily from the impact. Davey just stared at it. It's not that he didn't know what it was. He knew exactly. It was a water cooler bottle. Replacing the empty ones in his parents' home office with full ones was one of his standard chores. Brando still wasn't quite big enough — or careful enough — to do it without spilling half a gallon on the floor.

But he didn't expect to head-butt one in the Gulf of freaking Mexico. It took him a few moments to figure out what it was doing there. Then he realized that it was trash, washed out to sea just like he had been. It was partly submerged and tilted on its side, maybe a third full of water. It rose up and over each little swell that washed past them. It was the same cheap kind of bottle that his parents had downgraded to recently. It was made of thin, transparent, blue-gray plastic instead of the thicker, bluer, more opaque plastic of the name-brand bottles.

Davey looked at its humpbacked profile, its neck pointing up just enough to keeps its open mouth above water. *Yep,* he thought. *That's the shape I thought was an island.* He felt like he'd just failed a test. He wasn't getting closer to an island. He was getting closer to a water cooler bottle. He was treading water again, his legs rubbery and spent. He made his right hand into a fist. Then he reached out and smashed down on the top of the bottle. Stupid bottle!

The force of the blow pushed the mouth of the bottle underwater. Ocean water poured in. The neck tipped back up a moment later, and the bottle found its balance. It continued bobbing along on the water.

Davey did the same, but with more effort and a worse attitude. As his surprise faded, he made the obvious connection. He coughed up a single sharp laugh at himself for thinking a disposable plastic jug was an island. He was happy all of a sudden, almost overjoyed. *This thing floated!*

He leaned forward, kicked his legs, and grabbed the bottle. He hugged it with both arms. Love would not have been too strong a word. Now, the big test: He stopped kicking his legs. He began to sink, taking the bottle with him. He angled the opening of the bottle up into the air. They kept sinking. He held his breath as his

67

mouth neared the water. The bottle stabilized. Most of it was underwater, but the neck stuck up alongside Davey's head. He glanced over. It looked like the periscope of a little plastic submarine. More important, it was keeping them both afloat.

He let go with one arm and smashed the water three times. The first two were just sheer happiness and relief. The third was more like, *In your face, ocean!*

And now that he was thinking a little more clearly, he realized that he could make this even better. He gathered the little strength he had left. As tired as he was, it felt great. Because he knew he'd be able to rest after this, at least for a little while.

He waited for a little swell to pass. The bottle carried him up and over. Then he reached down and grabbed the bottom of the bottle. His mouth and nose dipped under the surface, so he moved fast. He lifted the bottle up and out of the water, kicking fiercely. His whole head was underwater now. Everything was under the water except his arms and the bottle. Above the little waves, he tipped the bottle down.

He tipped it down the same way he did when he replaced one in the office: just enough. It began to empty but stayed above the surface. He heard the splash of water on water. He wished that it really was full of bottled water, instead of salty brine. He would've drunk it all. As the bottle emptied, it became lighter. Even as his kicks grew weaker, they lifted him farther out of the water. Soon, his head was above the surface again. Then his shoulders were.

Then he was holding a big empty bottle, way up in the air. The sun was shining through it, making crazy patterns.

He flipped it back around, top up, and dropped it back in the water. It floated higher now. Even when he grabbed hold again, it floated higher. Even when he allowed his tired legs to stop kicking, it floated higher. The top third of the thing was above the surface. He leaned down and rested his head along the top and his cheek along the neck. This didn't solve anything. He knew that. He flicked his eyes forward and still saw nothing but a hazy blur of horizon.

But right at that moment, he didn't care. Right at that moment, and for quite a few after it, he rested. He hugged the big plastic bottle tight — his own little island — and rested.

15

The Tserings were nearing the far tip of the island when they realized someone was chasing them. He wasn't exactly running after them; it was more of an urgent walk that occasionally broke into an awkward jog. Brando was the first to notice.

"I think that guy from the hotel is after us," he said.

His parents turned and looked. Once they recognized him, they stopped and waited for him to catch up. There was nothing around. Just the ocean on one side of the walkway and the far corner of the hotel grounds on the other. There were no other people, and the only sounds came from the small waves and gentle breeze.

Once he'd been spotted, Marco slowed down. He tried to act casual as he walked toward them, but the sweat on his forehead gave him away. He gave them a small wave. Then he reached up to wipe his forehead in an exaggerated way, trying to make a joke out of it.

Word had gotten back to him at the main desk that there was a family out beating the bushes for a lost boy. That was not, in any way, good for business. He was in charge of things today. The owners of the hotel would have his hide if this blew up. Every advertisement they ran, from the brochures at the airports to the header on the website, used the phrase *family friendly*. He didn't want to spend the next year answering the phone and saying, "Oh, no, we hardly ever lose children. A very small percentage, really." And he didn't want all of the families checking out today going back home saying, "The craziest thing happened at the Aszure Island Inn. A boy just disappeared!" He didn't want the families checking in to worry about it the whole time, either. He needed to help this family find their kid — and hopefully get them to shut up about it until they did.

Pamela was looking at him like he was a stray dog. He wished he hadn't gotten off to such a bad start with her. It was hard to undo a bad first impression. He plastered on a big, toothy smile and gave them another wave. Only Brando waved back.

"Did you find him?" asked Tam hopefully.

Pamela perked up a bit. The possibility hadn't occurred to her.

Marco just shook his head. Tam and Pamela turned away from him to hide their disappointment, but Brando watched him closely.

"I should've gone the other way around," said Marco. "Just walked three-quarters of the island trying to catch up."

"Well, if you don't have any news, why did you bother?" asked Pamela.

Marco looked at her. *Big smile,* he told himself. "Wanted to help you look!"

"Wanted to shut us up, probably," said Pamela.

A bad attitude and smart, too, thought Marco. *How am I going to handle this one?* His smile flickered and then fell from his face.

"We both want the same thing," he said. "Any idea where he might've gone?"

Brando looked from his mom to Marco and back again. She seemed satisfied with his answer.

"No," said Pamela.

"And you've checked . . ." Marco made a little circle with his left hand.

"Yes," said Tam, "we've checked everything up to here."

"Everything?" said Marco.

"Every last grain of sand," said Tam.

Marco was sure that included asking every last person they came across. He cringed at the thought.

"Well, might as well keep going," he said, pointing down the walkway with his chin.

They continued on in the direction they'd been heading. They had an extra person now, but not much use for him. Brando looked around. This part of the island was even quieter — and that was saying something. There were no bar stands or docks, no little clusters of people. In their place was an extra helping of trees and scrubby little bushes. He watched as Marco made a show of helping. He leaned over to look behind a tree and then leaned back to look up into it.

"My brother isn't a monkey," said Brando.

Marco looked down and flashed his big smile at him, but Brando wasn't buying it.

"Where does this little path go?" said Pamela. She was a few steps ahead of the rest of them and pointing down at a little gap in the undergrowth.

"Goes to a little beach," said Marco.

"We should check it out," said Tam, but Marco had already caught up with them and started down the path.

Without another word, they turned and followed him. It was a narrow path, and they had to walk single file to avoid the saw grass. Marco moved quickly, barely looking down. He knew the path well. Hotel employees sometimes hid out back here, extending their breaks as long as they thought they could get away with. *It is definitely a place a kid could go and not be noticed,* he thought.

But when they reached the mouth of the path, there was no one there. No employees, and no missing boy. Brando pushed past him on the left as Tam and Pamela pushed past him on the right. He followed a few steps behind, and they all fanned out across the little beach.

"Davey!" called Pamela.

"You here, champ?" called Tam. "Where are you? We're not mad!"

Brando let out a little burst of air. *Yeah, right,* he thought. But his eyes scanned every inch of the beach.

They all noticed the same things in a different order. Brando saw the No Swimming sign and then scanned the line of surf. Pamela scanned the surf first and then saw the sign. Tam was still staring into the deep shadows along the trees at the beach's edge and nearly tripped over the thing. He read it.

"He's not, uh . . ." Marco began, nodding toward the sign. He didn't even want to think it, much less say it. But he had to. "Your son, he's not much of a swimmer, is he?"

Pamela looked at him, horrified.

"No!" she said. She disliked him more now, just for saying that.

"No, he used to, but he doesn't even . . ." said Tam. He was distracted, just now scanning the surf. He snapped out of it when he finished. "No, he used to go to the lake, but I don't think he went at all last year." He turned to look at Brando. "You guys go to the lake last summer?"

"Not much. Maybe twice," said Brando. "He never wanted to."

What he didn't say was that he still wasn't allowed to go alone. His parents already knew that, and Marco figured it out from his tone of voice.

"Yeah, Davey's in more of an indoor phase right now," said Tam. "And he definitely wouldn't ignore a sign like this, either."

"That's true," said Brando. In the last year or two, his brother had become the sort of freak kid who walked around fences instead of climbing over them.

"You should get a new sign," said Pamela, frowning at the faded letters. "Or at least stand it up straight."

"Not hotel property," said Marco.

"I don't care whose property it is," she said, looking directly at him. Marco looked down and saw an old cigarette butt in the sand. He had an eagle eye for them at this point. He looked around, wondering if there was anything else he was missing.

Brando saw his eyes searching the ground and did the same. It occurred to him to look for footprints, but the beach was full of them now. Four fresh sets. He looked up and tried to see the beach the way Davey would. It was quiet, and there was shade over by the trees. It would be a good place to sit and read.

"He'd like it here," he said. But the adults were still squabbling about who did or did not own the beach and didn't hear him. He went up to where the first trees met the sand. He stood under one. Then he sat down. He positioned himself so that his legs were in the sun and the rest of him was in the shade. He pretended he had a book in his lap.

"Come on, Brando," called Tam. "You can rest at the hotel later."

Brando looked over. They were back at the mouth of the little path. He took a quick look at the bushes and trees behind him.

Even with the sun burning bright overhead, they were stuffed with shadows. He looked closer. "Davey?" he said.

There was no response. He stood up and brushed the sand off his shorts. Twenty yards away, the grown-ups started back down the path. Brando hurried to catch up.

16

Drew was waiting in line at the breakfast buffet. She was going to get one of those big meaty American meals she'd heard about. The smell of bacon wafted her way, and her stomach rumbled for it. She'd barely eaten anything since she'd arrived on the island. She was beginning to wonder if she ever would. So far all she had on her plate was silverware and a stiff cloth napkin. Her dad was talking to the guy in front of them and holding up the works.

"You can't have just one slice of bacon!" said the man. He had some sort of accent. Drew ran through the different sorts of American accents she knew, all from movies or TV. She pegged this guy as either a cowboy or a redneck, possibly both.

"Now hold on a minute!" said her dad. "I'm watching my boyish figure!"

She could hear him making his own accent bigger, playing to his audience. She rolled her eyes. *Come on,* she thought.

"Well I'm sorry to say that horse has left the barn," said the man. Now Drew was thinking cowboy, just because of the horse thing. Her father laughed. The "horse" was his boyish figure. It had gotten away. Boy, had it. Everything about Big Tony was big these days, and that included his stomach.

"That a Texas accent?" asked Big Tony.

"Louisiana," said the man.

Drew wasn't exactly sure where that was, but she knew it wouldn't matter. Her dad would just pretend the guy was from Texas, anyway. She looked at the man. All he had on his head was a bald spot, but it would be a giant cowboy hat when her dad told the story. *This big bloke from Texas told me to have more bacon. Had to oblige before he drew his pistols!*

She could reach the scrambled eggs from where she was, but she held off. If she put them on her plate now, they'd just get cold. She could already tell the other man was just like her father: a big talker. There was no telling how long this would go on. She let out a long sigh. It contained as much annoyance as air, but no one heard it. The man was talking again.

"How about you? That's not a Liverpool accent you're slinging around, is it?"

Oh no, now he's done it, thought Drew.

"I'm no bleeding Liverpudlian!" bellowed her father. She could practically hear heads all over the dining room turning to look. So embarrassing. "I'm a Mancunian to the core!"

"You live in . . . Manchester?" said the man.

Her father raised his eyebrows. He was impressed. "Just outside," he said. "Manchester's not a place you live. It's a place you come from and go back to for football."

Drew watched as the man nodded. She could tell he was still picking the words out of her dad's thick accent.

"That's soccer to you," he added, but it wasn't necessary.

"United or City?" said the man.

Here we go, thought Drew.

"United!" thundered her dad. She risked a look over her shoulder. There weren't that many people in the dining room yet, but they were all either looking over or, worse, making an effort not to. "When I die, my face'll turn red, not blue!" her dad was saying, referring to the colors of the two teams.

Drew picked her plastic tray up off the metal railings. This had gone on long enough.

"Seen a few games myself," said the man. "They show them here on —"

Drew dropped her tray down onto the railings. *BANG!*

The man looked over. "Looks like the natives are getting restless," he said.

Drew had no idea what that meant.

"This one's always restless," said her father. He reached over to ruffle her hair, but she ducked him. She wasn't ten anymore! "This is my daughter, Drew."

"David," said the man. "I was just telling your old man here to have more than one slice of bacon."

"You can bet I'm going to," she said. Then she bumped her dad's tray with hers.

The men laughed. Her dad took two more strips of bacon.

"There you go," said David. And amazingly, there they went, filling up their trays with bacon and eggs, some sort of potato thing, and the odd piece of fruit.

"Come on over and sit with us," said David, as they neared the end of the buffet. "My wife and I have that big table all to ourselves."

"Right," said her dad. "Go get your mum, will you, luv?"

Drew looked over at her mom, sitting alone at another table. She'd had the good sense to beat her husband to the buffet line and was already halfway done with her food. Drew headed over.

"Dad's made a friend," she said. "From Louisiana."

Kate chuckled. "I heard."

"Whole room did," said Drew. But now that she had her food, she really didn't mind. She waited as her mom gathered up her things. Then they went over and sat at the new table. Introductions were made all around.

Drew began eating immediately. The bacon was wonderful. She didn't worry about talking. She knew it would be taken care of. There were two men at the table who very much enjoyed the sound of their own voices. She wondered who would go first. Maybe her dad would want to keep talking about Manchester United. It was by far his favorite topic.

But no, it was David who began. He wanted to talk about a missing boy.

"Just up and vanished from the room this morning, apparently," said David. "Just gone. Poof! And now his parents are out circling the island, calling his name."

"His name is David, too," added the wife, Julia.

"Yes, that's right," said David. "Just a little guy. Very sad. His parents, even his little brother, they're out there asking if anyone's seen him."

Drew put down her fork. More dropped than put down, actually. It clattered against the plate.

"Yes, luv?" said Kate.

Drew looked around the table and realized everyone was looking at her.

"Think I saw 'im," she said.

Big Tony looked at the empty air ahead of him, as if he kept all his memories floating there. "Yeah, that's right," he said. He nudged Kate. "Remember?"

She nodded slowly and looked over at her daughter. "You're right, luv," she said.

But they were talking about two different boys.

17

Davey clung tightly to the water cooler bottle. It wasn't that he thought it would go anywhere; it didn't look like either of them would. It just felt reassuring to have something else that was solid in all this endless water. A little swell came and he let the bottle carry him up and down again. His legs hung down, pointing straight into the deep. The sun was hitting him square. It was hitting everything out here.

Now that he didn't have to work constantly just to stay afloat, he could think more clearly. Mostly, he was thinking about rescue. He was sure his family had noticed he was gone by now. He was wondering if they would find his things on the beach, or if someone else would.

He ran over other ways that people might figure out what had happened to him. Someone else could get caught in the same rip current. It would have to be someone who knew what to do and could make it back to shore. Then they might report it. Then people might search the beach more closely, might find his things. Might, might, might.

The odds were bad. He knew that. He wasn't stupid. But he floated there stringing together events that could lead to his rescue. He did it for the same reason he hugged the bottle. It was comforting. And if he thought about it hard enough, he could almost believe it.

He scanned the skies for rescue planes. He listened closely for a helicopter. For one amazing moment, he thought he heard one. But it was only the gentle churn and chop of the ocean.

He scanned the horizon. His eyes were too weak to see land in the distance. But now that he had something solid to hold on to, he thought he could feel himself drifting. Maybe he'd drift into range. Or maybe he'd see a boat. A big tanker, a fishing boat, a Navy ship . . . He wasn't picky. But he saw nothing.

Davey was nearsighted, which meant he could see things close to him. He looked down and was surprised to see a little fish. It was the size of a goldfish, but a plain gray color. It was hanging in the water just in front of him, a foot or two below the surface. As he looked, he saw another. As he watched that one, he saw a third, partly hidden by his shadow.

"Little guppy guys," said Davey. He was speaking mostly to himself, but to tell the absolute truth, partly to the fish. It came out as a raspy croak. He knew his mouth was dry, but he had no idea his voice was so bad. He gathered up some spit. It tasted like salt. Somehow, he'd even gotten some sand in his mouth.

He spat into the ocean. One of the fish came up to investigate.

"Gross," said Davey, and he sounded better this time. He made a mental note to use his voice every now and then. He needed to keep it in working order in case that Navy ship arrived.

The fish dipped its head and flapped its tail, powering back down to its friends. Davey watched them for a while. He'd spotted a fourth now. They were hanging out under the water cooler bottle. *For the shade,* he thought, *or maybe the shelter.*

The truth is, small fish follow floating objects in the open ocean for both reasons. These ones had probably been following the bottle long before Davey showed up. But it was even better now. Much of the sunlight shined through the bottle, but Davey cast solid shade. And there were other advantages.

Davey felt a little tickle on one of his toes. He didn't think much of it. He'd been in the water for a long time now, and his whole body felt a little weird. His fingers were beyond pruned. But then he felt another little tickle. He looked down through the crystal clear water and saw one of the little fish in front of his foot.

Davey pulled his foot away. The little fish advanced slowly, maintaining about an inch of distance. It looked like it was locked in a staring contest with his big toe. And then it swam up and took a quick nibble. Davey felt the familiar tickle.

"Dude!" he said.

He kicked his foot hard. The fish retreated, its tiny mouth still working on the flake of dead skin it had scavenged. The fish stayed under the bottle for a while, but a few minutes later he felt another tiny mouth at work. It was on his other foot this time. He couldn't tell if it was the same fish or if that one had somehow told the others about the new restaurant in town.

He shooed them away, pumping the water cooler bottle up and down over their heads like a piston and unleashing a few quick, choppy kicks. The fish swam off in a little diamond formation.

They stopped a few feet away. They just hung there in the water. Fish are not the smartest creatures, and it was quite possible that they'd already forgotten the whole thing. Then one of them saw the bottle again. The bottle and the boy and the little floating island they formed.

They all swam back to it. This time they approached in an uneven line, two slightly ahead, two slightly behind, like pawns advancing up a chessboard. Davey pumped the bottle again — down, up, down.

The little fish retreated and returned.

Davey gave up. He went back to thinking about rescue. But beneath him and all around, the percussive plastic thumps he'd made with the bottle were still carrying through the water. It was an odd sound out here, the sort that would attract attention.

18

David and Julia had quickly worn out their welcome, but Drew's family still hadn't been able to shake them. Now they were all leaving the restaurant together. Drew gave her mom a quick, worried glance: *Are they just going to follow us around all day?* It seemed possible.

Finally, her dad executed a daring escape move. He walked several steps past the elevator bank. David didn't so much as look over at it. He didn't break stride, and he certainly didn't stop talking. He'd barely stopped once he'd gotten going. It was a mystery how he'd been able to clean his plate without spraying the table with egg bits.

"Oops, just got to pop back up to the room," said Big Tony.

Drew smiled. *Well done,* she thought, and it was. David and his better half had already walked past the elevators. They couldn't claim they needed to use them now, too. It was a clean break. Almost.

"All righty," said David. His tone was breezy but forced. He was struggling to come to terms with the loss of his audience.

"We'll just be at the concierge desk. We've got some questions for that lady."

Good, go talk her ear off, thought Drew. *At least she gets paid for it.*

Julia flashed them a quick, slightly desperate smile. It was like she was secretly being held hostage and trying to communicate the fact with her teeth and eyes. She'd barely said a word during the meal. But now she surprised them all with some actual information.

"Oooh," she whispered. "That's them!"

She pointed over toward a group standing near the computer and printer set up along the wall for guests to use. She and her husband both made exaggerated bug-eyed expressions at exactly the same moment. *How about that?*

She's no hostage, thought Drew. And then, mercifully, they walked away. Drew and her parents stayed put, pretending to wait for the elevator.

"Gah, I thought he'd never leave," said Big Tony.

"Thought he'd never shut up," said Drew.

"Still hasn't," said her mom. She nodded over toward the concierge desk, where David was already peppering a stylishly dressed young woman with questions. In sharp contrast to the scene a few hours earlier, the lobby was fully staffed now, bustling with activity.

Their eyes landed back on the family of the missing boy, still waiting for the computer to free up. A quick look at their body language made it clear how impatient they were. A man with headphones on was seated at the lone computer, completely unaware. He was video chatting with what looked to Drew like a ball of frizzy hair in a dark room.

Drew was the first to figure out what they were doing. "They're waiting to print out a picture," she said. "Like a missing person advert."

Kate gasped.

"Shame, isn't it?" said Big Tony.

"We should say something," said Kate.

"Right thing to do and all that," said Big Tony. "Should we, uh, should we all go, then?"

"You go," said Kate, waving him on. It had always been understood that he was the most social, the one to talk to strangers. He was the one who'd gotten them trapped at a table with David, after all. Now he had to make good.

The elevator dinged and opened up. No one got out, and they let it close again.

"Go on, then," said Kate.

He walked slowly over.

Drew turned to her mom. "Bit awkward, isn't it?"

*   *   *

Brando stared at the back of the man's head. *How clueless can this guy be?* he thought. It was bad enough he was chatting away with this frizzy-headed, Muppet-looking woman. It was much worse that they had to hear him do it. Brando fantasized about walking over and plucking the man's earphones right off. He couldn't decide what he'd do after that. Strangle him with the cord, maybe.

Brando looked around the lobby for what felt like the eighty-fourth time. This time, he saw a man heading straight for them. He was a big guy, and kind of tough-looking. He had a head that was either shaved or bald, maybe some of each, and a gut just shy of sumo-level.

Good, thought Brando. *If he wants to use the computer, too, maybe he'll body-slam lover boy here.*

"Pardon," he said.

Tam and Pamela turned around. Brando gave him a closer look. The man raised a big meaty hand and gave them a surprisingly dainty wave.

"Yeah, sorry to bother you," said Big Tony. His accent was so thick that all of the vowels seemed to be off by one. "My family and I . . ." He motioned over to two people standing by the elevator. Brando looked and saw a lady about his mom's age and a girl who looked like she might be in high school. He thought he could just see her bathing suit top through her shirt. He missed the next several sentences.

". . . so when we heard that, we thought we should let you know," Big Tony was saying when Brando tuned back in.

"Let us know what?" said Pamela.

"We saw the boy. Well, we saw *a* boy, anyway."

"When? Where?" said Tam.

"He was by himself," said Big Tony. Brando was paying close attention now. They all were. "He was down by the dock. Where the boat comes in, know what I mean? Just waiting there."

"Waiting for the boat?" Pamela said, a hint of panic rising in her voice.

Big Tony looked at her. "Couldn't say. Could be. He was just sitting there. We didn't think much of it, know what I mean? Called him a little pirate."

He had no idea why he'd added that part, but he couldn't unsay it now. Tam and Pamela looked at each other.

"Well, anyhow, thought you should know," he said, wrapping up.

"Yes, thank you!" said Tam. "Thank you so much."

Big Tony gave another little wave and started to retreat. At the last second, he changed his mind. He took a few quick steps forward. He reached down toward the man sitting at the computer and pulled the headphone away from the man's right ear.

"Hey! Chatty!" said Big Tony, louder now. "Time's up."

He let the headphone snap back. The man looked up, his expression shifting quickly from surprise to fear.

90

"Cool," said Brando, as Big Tony walked back toward the elevator.

"Did you tell 'em where he was?" asked Drew when her dad returned. In her mind, that was sitting under a tree by the bar stand, reading.

"Course," said Big Tony. In his mind, that was by the dock.

"Well done," said Kate. She meant ousting the man from the computer.

They were all on their own page, really. They didn't stick around as the missing boy's family printed out pictures from the newly available computer. They'd done their part. When the next elevator came, they took it.

On the short trip up to the fourth floor — the top floor of the hotel — Drew saw her opening. "We should take that boat into Key West today." She said it casually, as if the thought had just popped into her mind. "You know, just for a few hours. Then we'll know if we like it or not."

She thought they'd shoot her down immediately, but they didn't say anything at first. She held her breath as her parents looked at each other. As the elevator door dinged open, her dad shrugged. "Guess we might," he said. "Kind of depressing around here, kids disappearing and all that."

"I don't know," said her mom. "I was hoping for some quiet today."

Drew had an answer for that. "Good way to get rid of that David, isn't it?"

Check and mate. Kate conceded with a nod.

"Just don't you go vanishing on us!" said Big Tony, and then they all disappeared into their suite.

19

Now that he'd had some time to watch the little fish, Davey decided that they were more silver than gray. Every now and then, one of them would turn and catch the sunlight streaming down through the water just right. It would flash a brilliant silver, then turn and flash again. Sometimes he didn't even see the fish, just the flash. As clear as the water was, the surface got in the way. It bent the light and obscured everything below it, especially when there were ripples or swells.

Then he made a discovery. He was resting his head against the water cooler bottle, as he had been for a while. He usually looked around it, scanning for the boats that refused to show, for the land that refused to appear. But this time he looked through it. He thought maybe it would act like the lens of his glasses. Instead, it worked like the glass sides of a fish tank. Looking below the waterline, everything was much clearer.

Davey used it as a funky sort of swim mask. He tilted it forward and looked down. One of the little fish swam by. It grew slightly as it passed the middle of the bottle and then slipped by. Davey tilted the bottle more and found it again, swimming down to join its friends.

He spent some time watching them. They looked a little blurry, because the bottle wasn't perfectly clear. But apart from that, he had a good view. They made small moves in unison. They'd all turn to the right and then back to the left, or vice versa. Or they'd swim up a few inches and then back down. There didn't seem to be any reason for the moves, but they did them together, like a tiny boy band.

He shifted his body down a little lower in the water. It improved his view, but soon he felt a shiver go through him. As warm as the water was — close to eighty degrees — it was still twenty degrees below normal body temperature. The more time he spent in it, the more obvious that became. He scooted himself back up the bottle. He grabbed it near the top and pushed it farther down into the water.

The sun hit his back again. It took just a few minutes to burn the water off and start warming him up. He felt the skin there getting tight and knew he was already beginning to burn. But what choice did he have? He needed the heat.

He looked up at the sun. Was it directly overhead? Not quite, he decided. He realized he could tell the time with it. He was pretty sure that straight overhead meant noon. He decided it was around eleven o'clock. *That's it?* he thought. It felt like he'd been out here for twice that long. He wondered how long it would've felt like if he hadn't found the bottle. He wondered if he'd still be feeling anything at all.

He looked up at the sun again. It flashed like the biggest silver fish there ever was. Could he use it to figure out directions, too? A phrase flashed through his head: *rises in the east, sets in the west.* But he couldn't make it work because he couldn't figure out which way he was facing. Or if he was facing a different direction now than he had been five minutes ago. There were no fixed points to go by. There were a few clouds, way up, but they were moving, too. And he was being carried. He was sure of it now. He was drifting along in some larger current.

Is this the Gulf Stream? he wondered. He didn't think so; not yet.

He was sure about one thing, though: It didn't matter which direction was which when it was the sea deciding where he went.

As the sun continued to crawl across the sky, Davey went back to looking for boats or land. He went back to listening for helicopters or planes. The report came back the same each time: none, none, none, and none.

20

The only subject that was even half as interesting to Davey as rescue was this: What had he done wrong? He kept picking at the question like a scab. And it was a big scab, because he'd made a lot of mistakes.

Should he have stayed in bed? Yes. Could he have read his book there, even with the snoring and toxic gas? Yes. Did those things seem like dumb reasons to sneak away now? Of course.

But he had.

So should he have left a note in the room? No, he decided. He'd meant to be back before anyone woke up. And he wouldn't have known about the beach then anyway, so what good would a note have done?

Should he have stayed out of the water? One thousand percent yes. Had the sign told him to? Yes! Duh! *Oh my God, I'm an idiot!* For a while, that seemed like his biggest mistake. He beat himself up about it pretty badly. And then, just floating there and feeling like an idiot, he thought of a bigger mistake.

He was remembering the moment he gave up, how he'd been thinking about his dad giving up in that river. It reminded him of something, and then it was all so obvious.

A few months after the family had gotten home from the tubing trip, his dad tried to buy something called a never-ending pool. His mom had said it was because he was embarrassed that he "couldn't swim to that stupid tube." His dad would only admit that he "needed more regular exercise."

He still remembered the exact words because it had been one of his parents' first big fights. It had still been a new thing. Davey and his brother — still Brandon then — could hear it all, even though they were upstairs and their parents were downstairs.

The business had just started to go bad then, to "slow down." That was another thing he knew from those first arguments — and from a lot of the ones since then. In any case, things weren't going well, and they'd just gone on a vacation. His mom wouldn't let his dad buy the little pool.

Tam had gone to the showroom anyway, one day when Pamela was out. He'd taken Davey and Brandon. Even at the time, Davey knew his dad was trying to get them on his side. They brought their swimsuits and tried it out. Except for Brandon. The salesman said he was still too young. Anyway, it was kind of cool.

It was like a little tiny pool, not much bigger than a person. It had a motor at the front that created this powerful current, like one continuous wave. And you just swam against it and swam against it and swam against it for exercise. You could swim for an hour and not get anywhere but healthy. Well, if you could swim for an hour you were probably already super healthy, but that was the point of it. Davey had only lasted a few minutes, and that was after the salesman had turned the motor down for him.

He hadn't thought about it much after that day. He was pretty sure they'd never get one. His mom had only said they'd talk about it "once the business came back." They'd never talked about it again.

But now he wished they'd gotten the stupid thing. He wished they'd sold the minivan to pay for it. Because if he'd done it more than once, he would've remembered. You could swim forever and never reach the end of that thing. That's why they called it a never-ending pool. But all you had to do was take a few quick strokes to the side to reach the edge. That's how you got out.

He felt so stupid.

He'd swum against the rip current, trying to reach the end. He should've swum sideways. That's how you got out. He felt like someone had just kicked him in the stomach. And worse, he felt like he deserved it.

He tilted the bottle down. He watched the fish for a while, trying to distract himself from himself. He found three of them quickly and was looking for the fourth. That's when he saw it. It was farther down. It was hard to say how far. Maybe twenty feet, he thought. It was the quick flick of a tail, the black flash of an eye.

This was no little fish.

21

Holy cow, they're calling the cops, thought Brando.

A wave of hot panic nearly knocked him down. *They're going to question me. They're going to find out that I knew he was gone and went back to sleep. Should I just tell them now? Should I just tell Mom and Dad before the police arrive, before it's* . . . He searched his head for the phrase, the one they used on TV. *Before it's a* criminal matter?

He looked up at his parents. If either one of them had looked down at that moment, he would've told them. But they didn't. They were both busy. His dad was taping another picture of Davey to the wall. It was a digital picture Pamela had emailed to one of her friends. It was the first and best one they could find, and they'd cut it in half to crop out Brando. Now the oddly shaped photo — a tall rectangle with one sloping side — was centered on plain white paper. Underneath it read:

MISSSING BOY

DAVEY TSERING

PLEASE CALL!

The hotel's main number was under that, followed by their room number, since there was no cell phone service out here. No one had noticed the extra *S* in *missing* before they hit print. Fifty pages later, no one cared that much.

Brando looked over at his mom. She was talking to the hotel manager, Marco. He'd resurfaced as soon as they'd started taping up the flyers. Brando could tell he didn't like it. Every time they put one up, Marco gave them a look like they were spray-painting swear words onto the wall. For a while, Brando kept a close eye on him to make sure he didn't take the flyers right back down.

"The island doesn't have any police," Marco was saying.

"You have to have police," said Pamela.

"The island doesn't have its *own* police," Marco clarified. "We call Key West if there are any . . ." He let his voice trail off, not sure how to finish the sentence.

"Well, that's good!" said Pamela.

Why is that good? thought Brando. *In what possible way could that be good?* Then he remembered: Key West. That's where they thought he'd gone. That was their new "theory," because of what the big English dude had told them. That he'd seen a boy waiting by the boat dock early this morning.

That didn't sound right to Brando. It didn't seem like something Davey would do. He looked around. He could see close to a dozen of their flyers from where he stood. There were four on the front doors alone: two facing out, two facing in. *If he's still on the island, that oughta do it,* he thought.

"Do I just dial 9-1-1?" asked Pamela, holding up her phone.

"That won't work here," said Marco. He let out a long breath. "You can use the phone at the desk. I'll get the number."

"I could just dial 9-1-1," said Pamela as they headed toward the desk.

"Please don't," said Marco.

They kept talking after that, but Brando couldn't hear them. Everyone in the lobby was talking. Every time Brando looked around, he caught people staring. He knew what they were talking about.

His dad finished putting up a flyer. He'd used long strips of Scotch tape on all four edges, with extra strips in the corners. If a hurricane came through, the roof would blow off, but these flyers would still be up.

"Where'd everyone go?" said Tam.

"To call the cops," said Brando.

His dad nodded his head. "Good."

If Brando was going to tell him anything, this would've been the time. But he didn't, and the time passed. Ten minutes later, they were heading back to the little dock. Tam and Pamela looked at the ground carefully as they approached, as if they were tracking a wild animal, as if they knew how. Finding no Davey tracks, they stepped onto the dock.

Tam tried to put up a flyer on one of the thick wooden pilings, but it was too breezy and the wrong kind of tape. They headed for the far end of the dock. There were no other people waiting because another boatful had just left.

Marco stayed behind on the sand, talking quietly into a little walkie-talkie. Brando was sure he was telling someone to take down all the flyers. He stared hard at the little yellow walkie-talkie. He wished he had Magneto's powers, or Jedi powers maybe. He'd crush the thing with his mind. He tried anyway. Nothing. Marco kept whispering, and the thing kept delivering little bursts of static in response.

Brando headed down the dock to join his parents. He looked over at the bar guy's battered, lopsided boat as he passed it. He wished he could just take it and go searching for his brother, but he knew that wouldn't end well. Instead, he waited with his parents. They didn't have to wait long.

Brando sat down on the end of the dock. He let his legs hang over the end and wasn't even all that curious why he felt his butt getting wet. It was a dock, after all. As soon as he looked up, he saw the little powerboat heading their way.

It knifed through the water in a straight line at first. Then it began arcing toward the dock, like an arrow on the way down. The boat bounced crisply over the little six-inch swells and left a long white wake behind it. Despite everything that was going on, despite all the bad things, Brando couldn't help but think: *That's frickin' awesome.*

As the police launch got closer, Brando could make out more details. It looked like an inflatable orange boat made permanent, with a metal frame reflecting the sun and a little cockpit in the center that looked just big enough for a person to stand up in. Soon, he saw the outline of the man's head and shoulders through the little window.

The man cut the motor and the boat drifted the last fifty yards to the dock. The launch bounced lightly against one of the tires hanging down along the pilings. The man stepped out from the little cockpit, picked up a line, and secured the boat. He pulled himself up onto the dock.

"Morning," he said.

Tam and Pamela said hello, but Brando didn't respond. He'd never seen a police officer in shorts before. He looked back down at the boat, just to make sure it was an official police boat. The words stenciled on the side in white spray paint seemed to leave no doubt about that, and there was a flasher and siren on top of the cockpit.

He looked back up at the guy. He looked young. Not like a kid, but not 100 percent like an adult, either. His shorts were hitched up too high, and he had a sunburn. It wasn't a tan, like Marco and most of the other people who worked on the island. It was a burn, like he was a tourist himself. A spray of messy blond hair stuck out from under his police cap. *This is the guy they sent?* thought Brando. *He looks like a Cub Scout troop leader.*

Marco thumped loudly down the dock, his dress shoes pounding the wood. He was still stuffing the walkie-talkie into his pocket with his left hand as he reached over with his right to shake the young cop's hand. "Hey, Jeff," he said. "Sorry to drag you out here on a Sunday."

Oh, great, thought Brando, *they know each other.*

He tried to use his mind powers again, even though he was pretty sure he didn't really have them. This time he was going for less Magneto, more Professor X. Jedi would still work, too. He thought as loud as he could: *Come on, Davey. Where are you? This isn't funny anymore. It was never funny. You need to get back here.*

The adults began to talk all at once. Brando stood alone on the edge of the dock. All he could see was clear blue water.

Where are you?

22

Davey was two and a half miles offshore, drifting to the southwest in a countercurrent. It was a bad situation, and it had just gotten worse.

That was a shark. He was sure of it now.

He replayed the images in his head. There was the first quick one, just a blur as it turned quickly and vanished. If that had been it, he could've told himself it was something else. It could've been some other big fish, a tuna maybe. But then he'd seen it again. It was moving slower this time. It was in no hurry at all, and why should it be? This was its home, not Davey's.

It glided slowly by, ten feet down. He saw its pointed head and its knifelike body. The water and plastic between them warped its shape slightly as it slid by, but he followed it and got a good look. He could see its fins, as clear as any nightmare he'd ever had. The dorsal fin angled straight up like a sail; the pectoral fins projected out like wings. Its mouth hung just slightly open, a line of black in all that blue.

He lost sight of it. He turned the bottle, tugged it through the water, tilted it farther down. Nothing, it was gone again. He began to see stars and realized he'd been holding his breath the whole time. He gulped in air and tried again. This time he dunked his head under the water and tried it without the bottle. He opened his eyes, but all he saw was water.

The little fish had scattered, not because of the shark but because Davey was moving the bottle all over the place. He saw them now, just off to his left. They were four little gray blurs, moving in unison. They skittered a few feet farther away as he watched them. *It's behind me!* he thought.

He jerked his body around, kicking his legs and pushing through the water with his right arm. His left arm was draped over the top of the water cooler bottle, and it was slowing him down. *By the time I see it, it will have its teeth in me.*

But when he completed his turn, there was nothing there. The endless ocean faded to a featureless blur in front of him. The ocean pressed in. He let out a few bubbles to keep the salt water out of his nose. He looked to his left, to his right, and then down past his feet. He surfaced, blowing out air as he went.

He checked to make sure no water had gotten into the bottle during the commotion. He wanted to climb up on top of the thing. He wanted to stand on it, like a lumberjack rolling a log. But he couldn't. It would sink, and then where would he be?

He told himself to calm down, not to panic. Yes, it was a shark, but it was small. It didn't look much more than three feet long. There was no way to be sure at that distance, but that's what he decided: three feet. Four feet, tops. He was taller than it was. *I'll punch it in the face if it tries anything!* That made him feel better.

For a while, he alternated between scanning under the water for the shark, scanning the horizon for boats, and scanning the sky for a plane or helicopter. He made them Official Survival Tasks and kept himself busy with them. He thought about how he'd signal if he saw a boat: He'd wave the bottle, splash around, shout as loud as he could. Same for a plane, he decided, except there wouldn't be any point in shouting.

The worst of his panic subsided, but his nerves were still stretched as tight as guitar strings. He heard a splash off in the distance, and it was like someone had strummed those strings with a hammer. He whipped his head around but saw nothing.

He wanted to scream, more out of frustration than fear. He had no idea what had caused the splash. Had something jumped out of the water? Why? He forced himself to go back to his Official Survival Tasks. Task 1: Look for shark. Task 2: Look for boats and/or land. Task 3: Look for planes and/or helicopters. Task 1: Look for shark. . . . Half an hour later, he had one other task to take care of.

Davey was the kind of kid who got out of the water to go to the bathroom under normal circumstances. These were not normal circumstances. The little fish had returned, and he apologized to them as the water got ever so slightly warmer.

It's hard to say he'd just made an enormous mistake. What choice did he have, really? Still, sharks are legendary for their sense of smell. Less well known: the fact that urine in the water is nearly as intriguing to them as blood.

Eventually, there would be that, too.

23

"You'd be the family of the boy, then," the officer was saying.

Brando noticed that he didn't say *missing* boy. Everybody noticed that.

"Yes, I'm Tam Tsering, his father."

"I'm Pamela Marcum Tsering, his mother."

The officer pulled a notebook out of his pocket. Brando had seen a hundred cops do that on TV. They'd pull a little notebook out of the back pocket of their pants or, if they were detectives, the inside pocket of their sports coat. This guy pulled it out of the side pocket of his cargo shorts.

"Well, I'm Jeff Fulgham. Deputy Jeff Fulgham — always forget that part. You can call me Jeff, Deputy, whatever you're comfortable with."

He was fishing around in his pocket again. This time he came up with a pen, but he didn't write anything. He turned toward Marco and asked, "What time's the next boat?"

Marco looked down at his watch. "Twenty minutes," he said. "Or whenever Zeke gets here."

"Yeah," said Deputy Fulgham. "This isn't the best place. People are going to start lining up, anyway. Let's go somewhere to talk."

"We can go out back by the pool," said Marco. "Nice place to sit. Should be quiet."

Who cares if it's a nice place to sit? thought Brando, but no one was asking him. The deputy hadn't even asked him his name.

They were all rumbling back down the dock now. Marco and the deputy were in the lead, talking low. Brando picked up his pace a little. He wanted to get close enough that he could hear what they were saying, but not close enough that they'd notice him. He watched the handle of the deputy's gun move back and forth as he walked. The gun was black, and so was the holster. When Brando looked closely, he could see the long rectangular edge of the magazine.

But he couldn't hear what they were saying. The footsteps, the breeze, the distance . . . They all conspired to keep things secret.

It took them just a few minutes to arrive at the pool. Deputy Fulgham looked around and pointed at a table. It had a glass top, a beach umbrella built right in, and five seats: just the right number. Tam and Pamela filed past and took seats next to each other. Brando took a few steps and then knelt down next to Marco and the deputy and pretended to tie his sneaker. He listened closely and heard the last words Marco said: ". . . no divers. Please. Not yet."

No divers? What does he mean by that? But Brando barely had time to think about it, because Marco nearly tripped over him on his way to the little table. Deputy Fulgham headed over, too. Brando had untied his lace for his act and now he really did have to tie it. When he finished, he pulled out the last chair and sat down. The interview was already in progress.

"Can I keep this?" said the deputy. He was holding one of the flyers.

"Sure," said Tam. "Course."

"And how old is he?" said the deputy, folding the flyer.

"Thirteen," said Tam.

"And a half," said Pamela.

"So almost fourteen?" said the deputy.

Pamela just looked at him, like, *Obviously.* The deputy didn't notice. He was jotting something down in his little notebook. Brando looked over. He squinted. He thought he could just make out the first —

"What's your name, little dude?" said the deputy.

Brando looked up; the deputy was looking right at him. He was so startled that he nearly tipped his chair over backward. "Brando," he said.

"It's Brandon," said his dad.

Oh my God, thought Brando. *Did I just lie to the police?*

"He prefers Brando these days," said Pamela.

They were talking about him like he wasn't there. He hated that. *Also,* he thought, *did he just call me "little dude"?* He didn't feel guilty anymore. He felt mad.

"And how old are you?" said the deputy. Now he was talking too loud. Brando hated that, too. He hated when adults spoke LOUDLY and CLEARLY to him. How was that supposed to help? He wasn't seven — or deaf. His grandmother shouted at him, too, but he didn't mind that so much. She actually was deaf.

"I'M TWELVE!" he said.

"All right, little dude," said the deputy, jotting it down. "No need to shout." He turned back to Tam and Pamela, so he missed the look Brando gave him. The deputy had a talent for ducking looks.

"And when was the last time you saw" — Deputy Fulgham looked down at his notes — "Davey?"

"Last night," said Tam.

"When we went to bed," said Pamela.

"What time was that?"

"Around ten," said Tam. "Maybe ten thirty. It was a long day."

"You got in yesterday? From?"

"Yes," said Pamela. "From Cincinnati. We live right outside."

"And you were all in the one room?"

"Yes," said Tam.

"And you didn't notice he was missing until this morning?"

"No," said Tam.

"No," said Pamela.

And then everyone was looking at Brando. He felt his face getting hot. His stomach tightened up. Panic grabbed at him with a thousand sharp little fingers. But then he thought about the question, the actual words of it. The little fingers let go.

"No," he said. And that was true. He hadn't noticed Davey was missing until this morning. The deputy hadn't asked him *when* this morning.

"And what time was that?"

D'oh!

"About eight thirty," said Pamela.

Brando was stewing in his chair again. The umbrella built into the table was keeping the sun off them, but he still felt like he was in a microwave. The deputy didn't even look over at him, though. The microwave clicked off.

"So he could've left anytime after ten thirty last night?" said Deputy Fulgham. He looked over at Marco, who shook his head.

"There's someone at the desk until at least midnight."

"That when the bar closes?" asked the deputy.

"Yes," said Marco. "Kitchen closes at ten, but the bar stays open at least that late."

It was quiet for a few minutes as the deputy scribbled furiously in his notebook. Finally, he looked up. "Who was at the desk last night?"

"Debbie," said Marco. "Debbie Reyes. You know her."

"Oh yeah . . . And?"

"Nothing," said Marco. "Already called her. She remembers

114

checking them in, that's it." Brando remembered the lady who had checked them in: She was tall, and her hair was taller. "And she definitely would've noticed a boy wandering around by himself at that hour."

"Okay, so . . ." said the deputy. More scribbling.

"Listen, Deputy," said Tam.

The scribbling stopped. He looked up.

"Our son wouldn't . . . I mean, he wouldn't leave the room in the middle of the night. Where would he even go?"

"Right, right, of course," said the deputy. "Just trying to establish a time line here."

More scribbling.

"So you think it was this morning?"

"Yes," said Tam.

"Of course," said Pamela.

"Yes," said Brando. "He took his book."

"He took his what?"

But before Brando could repeat it, the loudest family on the face of the earth arrived. At least that's what they seemed like to Brando. It was two enormous adults and a little girl in water wings.

"Don't go in the pool yet!" called the man.

"Not yet, baby!" called the woman.

"I wanna go in the water!" shrieked the child.

"Now, you wait for Mommy!"

The whole table watched them. There was a brief cease-fire in all the yelling as the family began to unload their stuff next to the lounge chairs on the other side of the pool.

"Yes, this morning," said Pamela, tired of beating around the bush. "Someone saw him by the boat thing. . . . By the . . . the dock."

"What was that?" said the deputy, suddenly all ears. "Come again?"

"Yes," said Pamela, taking a deep breath before proceeding. "It was an English family. They told us in the lobby."

Behind them, there was a splash, a scream. "Don't go in the deep end!" called the little girl's mother.

No one paid them any mind. Deputy Fulgham was scribbling so hard, Brando was sure he'd tear the paper.

24

Davey hated the way that his legs hung down in the water. He hated, hated, hated it. He wasn't sure if he should keep his feet moving or keep them still. Specifically, he wasn't sure which was more likely to get them bitten off. He thought about fishing, as if his legs were the line and his feet were the bait. Did people just leave the bait hanging there, or did they move it around?

They did both. That was no help. He decided to keep doing what he'd been doing before he saw the shark: pushing his feet slowly back and forth underneath him. The bottle was enough to keep him afloat without that, but he had to hold on tight and pull it down lower into the water. He didn't want to be any lower than he had to be, so he kept kicking.

He looked down through the bottle almost constantly now. There was another little fish. It was bright blue, like a piece of candy, and seemed to come and go. The four silver-gray fish — his little guppy guys — didn't pay it much mind. They'd settled into a patch of water between the bottle and Davey's slowly churning feet.

Davey looked down and waited for the little blue fish to come back. It reminded him of an aquarium. He really liked that idea, like this whole thing was just a show for his benefit. He'd been to two aquariums, the one in Cincinnati and the one in Cleveland. They were both pretty good. His favorite thing was that his parents would let him and Brando run around on their own. I guess they considered it safe, with all of the aquarium employees walking around in their rubber boots and short-sleeve shirts. It was probably his parents' favorite part, too, now that he thought about it.

This was back when he and Brando still did everything together — the lake, the aquarium, bikes. So they'd run all over the place, looking for the turtles. His little brother really liked turtles. He liked all kinds, but especially the big sea turtles. He'd wait by the glass until one came all the way around the tank. Then he'd just watch it, mesmerized. Sometimes it seemed like the turtle was watching him, too. At least that's what he said.

Brando and his turtles, thought Davey. He smiled, just a little. And then he remembered the hat. The last time they'd gone, Brando had spent all his money on a dumb foam hat that looked like a turtle. It had a little turtle head on the front and foam flippers sticking out from the sides. He'd worn it home, even outside the aquarium.

The smile fell away. It had been one of the first times he'd been really, truly embarrassed to be around his younger brother. How old had he been? He tried to remember. He'd probably just turned twelve, so Brando would've still been ten.

Absolutely alone and miles from shore, he thought about that. *A ten-year-old in a turtle hat . . . so what?* Davey remembered how he'd quietly but relentlessly made fun of his brother in the backseat until he took the hat off. *God, what was my problem?* If Brando showed up right now, he could be wearing a turtle hat and a turtle skirt, for all Davey cared. Just so long as there was a nice sturdy boat underneath him.

The little blue fish was back. It swam right through the other fish. They moved aside to let it pass and then regrouped. Below them, a shark cruised into view. It startled Davey, and his body jerked backward. He stopped kicking his legs. He was pretty sure it was the same one as before, but he wasn't 100 percent sure. It's not like they'd been introduced. He held his breath and stayed still. He sank down half a foot, pulling the bottle down with him.

The shark curved slowly off to the right. He followed it just with his eyes until it reached the edge of the bottle. Then he took a breath and moved the bottle with his arms, just enough so that he could still see it. At first he thought it was moving away, but as he kept moving the bottle it kept reappearing.

It was moving in a circle. Both of the aquariums he'd been to had sharks. They'd moved in circles, too, but they had no choice. That was the shape of the tanks. This one had a choice.

There's a shark in my aquarium, thought Davey, *and it's circling me.*

It came close enough for him to get a good look at it through the plastic even without his glasses. It was a blue shark, long and thin, like the kids on the junior high basketball team. It was a dark blue shape in clear blue water, hard to keep track of. Its head came almost to a point, like a shark pen you'd buy in an aquarium gift shop. As it circled, Davey could see the large eye on the right side of its head. It was wide open, unblinking and black, like a hole in the sea.

When it began its second time around — or at least the second one he was aware of — Davey began to churn his feet again. It made it easier to follow along and keep an eye on the thing. The little gray fish scattered and regrouped, scattered and regrouped, annoyed by the activity. The bright blue one skittered back down into the deep. Davey just looked past them.

He followed the shark twice more around, the circle getting wider, then tighter. When it got wider again, he gave up. The shark could keep this up a lot longer than he could. It was exhausting, and he was already spent. He'd begun to shudder now and then. It was less from fear than from his dropping body temperature. A deep, feverish chill passed through him.

He hugged the bottle and pulled his legs up so that his thighs pressed against the flat plastic bottom. He sank down again. He used his arm muscles to try to keep the top of the bottle pointed straight up and the back of his head pointed at the warm sun overhead.

But his arms and shoulders ached. He couldn't keep this up, either. He thought about the sharks at the aquarium, how they circled and circled. How there were other things in the tank with them: little fish, rays, and smaller sharks. They didn't even seem to notice. And a ray — how easy a meal would that be for a shark? They just glided by like floating pancakes, and still none of them got eaten.

Davey thought about the little fish, completely unconcerned with the shark and just waiting for him to get his stupid legs away from their beloved floating bottle. Maybe this shark was like the fish. Maybe it was just curious about this strange thing on the surface, this Unidentified Floating Object. That made him feel a little better. It even allowed him to breathe a little more normally and let his legs relax down away from the bottle.

He chose not to think about the other part of that: that the first thing the little fish had done to check him out was give him a good nibble. He was pretty sure that if the shark did the same, he was done for. There'd be blood in the water, and then they'd all come.

He looked down through the bottle often. Sometimes he could see the blue shark, sometimes he couldn't. He looked back over his shoulder, he worried, but he told himself the same thing over and over: *They've been looking for me for hours now back on the island. That's plenty of time to find my stuff. And now that they've done that,* he told himself, *it'll be easy for them to figure out what happened. Maybe there's even a chart of the currents.*

He took another long look below, waiting until the shark came into view. Then he forced himself to go back to his old routine: scanning the horizon and checking the sky before finally letting himself look back down into the water.

Maybe the planes are already in the air, he thought.

Maybe the boats are already out searching the water.

But back on land, they were still sitting around the pool and talking.

Still just talking.

"Did you get his name?" asked Deputy Fulgham.

"No, we didn't get his name," said Pamela. "He was a big, huge Englishman and he came up to us and said he saw a boy alone by the boat dock."

"But you didn't get his name?"

"How many gigantic Englishmen can there be on this island?" said Pamela.

"I remember him," said Marco. "Asked me what time the restaurant opened for breakfast. It's him and his wife and a daughter, I think. Suite on the fourth floor."

"Remember his name?" said the deputy. His pen was poised over his little notebook.

"I can get it," said Marco.

"Who cares about his name?" Pamela said loudly. Her frustration was quickly turning into anger.

Brando flinched, remembering the times she spoke to him that way. He watched the deputy, interested to see how he'd respond. Fulgham put his pen down on the table and looked at her. "I'd like to ask him some questions, that's all," he said. He had a little smile on his face, as if she'd just told him a mildly amusing joke.

Brando was impressed. He knew it probably made his mom even madder, but it gave her no good reason to show it. That was so much smarter than getting mad back, which was what he usually did. Maybe he'd underestimated this Cub Scout leader.

Tam had seen the whole thing, too. He knew his wife was getting angry and tried to step in. "It seems like the important thing is that Davey was by the docks early this morning," he said. "This guy — whatever his name is — told us that plain as day."

The deputy considered it. He had no reason to doubt him.

"All right," said Fulgham, "so you think he got on one of the boats and headed over?"

"Yes," said Pamela. She was calmer now, happier with where the conversation was headed.

"Why?"

"I don't know!" So much for her calmness. "He probably wanted to buy something else to read — he likes fantasy books and graphic novels. Or maybe he just wanted to take the boat back and forth. He probably just woke up early and was bored!"

"Okay, okay," said the deputy, putting his hand up in a stop sign. "I can see you've thought about this. And he's thirteen, right?

I know I did some crazy things when I was a teenager around here. Island life, man."

That last part didn't seem very helpful to Brando. And he didn't think his brother would do something like that, anyway. It's not that he hadn't changed now that he was a teenager; he just hadn't changed in that way. And he'd never been the hop-a-boat-to-party-city type. Brando decided to say something, but all he could come up with was: "He already has a book."

The deputy looked at him but didn't even write it down. He still had a far-off look on his face, thinking about that "island life." Finally, he snapped out of it. "Okay, okay," he said. "Hey, Marco, how much does Zeke charge for a ride these days?"

"Five dollars a head," said Marco. "But sometimes the kids slip on for free. He doesn't pay much attention."

"Well, there you go," said the deputy. "Did he have any money on him?"

"Yeah, sure," said Tam.

"He gets an allowance for his chores," said Pamela. "Extra for big ones."

"Not that much extra," said Brando. The deputy chuckled. Brando was starting to get as angry as his mom. They weren't listening to him. He wasn't complaining about his own allowance. He was saying that Davey wouldn't blow ten bucks for a round-trip boat ride.

And then Marco surprised everyone, himself included, by saying,

"I met the first boat when it came in." He was thinking it so hard that it just popped out of his mouth.

"Oh, yeah?" said the deputy, sitting up in his chair.

"What?" said Pamela.

"Yeah," said Marco, but what he was thinking was, *How am I going to dig myself out of this one?*

"Well," said the deputy, "did you see the kid?"

Marco let out a long breath. He picked one of the flyers up off of the table and looked at it. "I don't know," he said.

"What do you mean, you don't know?" said Pamela. "You either saw Davey or you didn't!"

Marco looked at her. He still didn't like her. "What I mean by 'I don't know' is I don't know, all right, lady? It was early, and there were definitely some boys there. Maybe a little younger, maybe a little older. I was looking at their hands more than their faces, just helping Zeke collect the fares."

"But you must've —" started Tam.

"Believe me, I've thought about it. I've looked at this picture about four hundred times now, and I want to say, yes, he was there. But I don't know if his face looks familiar because I saw it this morning or because it's been on every frickin' door I've walked through since you taped those things up."

"Unbelievable," said Pamela, waving her hand at him.

Marco shrugged. He was just telling the truth.

"Not very helpful, Marco, my man," said the deputy. "I'll tell you what, though. Why don't you run down there and tell Zeke I need a word with him. Next boat's got to be getting in soon. Maybe he's got a little better memory of things."

Marco doubted it. "Sure," he said, pushing out of his chair and standing up.

He headed toward the dock, but right away he ran into a little line of people heading up the walkway, luggage in hand. The boat was already here. Brando watched him break into a jog.

"Should we go with him?" said Tam. "It looks like the boat is already here."

"Well, hopefully Marco can lasso Zeke before it leaves," said the deputy. "Boat won't go anywhere without him. Meantime, let me just clear up a few other possibilities."

"What do you mean?" said Pamela.

"Just want to cross a few things off my list."

"Fire away," said Tam.

"All right, first of all, have you seen anyone weird hanging around since you've been here? Maybe someone Davey might've talked to?"

No one asked what he meant by *weird*. They all knew what he was getting at. Tam and Pamela looked at each other.

"No," said Pamela. "I keep an eye out for . . . people like that. We got in late: last boat. I don't even think it was this Zeke guy anymore, just some little boat. The lady checked us in, and we went straight to our room."

"We ordered room service," added Tam. "Guy didn't even come all the way into the room with the cart."

"Okay," said the deputy. "No red flags there. And this next one, it's not so much a vacation question, but it's standard. What do you do, you know, professionally?"

"We work together," said Pamela. "We run a business."

"What kind of business?"

"We import arts and crafts from Tibet," said Tam.

"Are you from there?"

"My family is," said Tam. "Originally."

"All right, so what kind of arts and crafts?"

"Handmade stuff," said Tam. "It's nice. A lot of religious-type stuff."

"How's business?"

Tam and Pamela both made faces.

"Not great," said Tam with a little shrug. "When we started out, we were just about the only people doing this. Now, well, we're not."

"So you have competitors."

"We do now," said Pamela.

"Any of them might have a grudge against you, anything like that?"

"I think most of them just . . . If anything, they probably feel a little sorry for us at the moment," said Tam.

Brando's mouth dropped open. He didn't know it was that bad.

"But you're here," said the deputy. "You can afford a nice vacation."

"We got a great deal," said Tam.

"And we needed a vacation," said Pamela. "The idea was some time with the family, some time to think about the business."

"Like how to fix it — the business, I mean," said the deputy.

Pamela looked at him, deciding how much to tell him. "Yes," she said. "I mean, like my husband said, a lot of what we sell is religious in nature, and we need to respect that. We can't just think of it as 'religious-type stuff.'"

"My bad," said Tam.

The deputy looked at him and then back at her. "So you think you're too, like, commercial?"

"And I think we're not commercial enough — it's still a business," said Tam. "She's the true believer. I'm the guy who left."

"Got it," said Fulgham. He paused to jot something down, and then looked up. "Ever argue about it?"

The table was quiet for a few moments. Finally, Pamela looked over toward the pool. "We just did, didn't we?"

The deputy looked over at Brando. Now he wanted his input. Brando gave him one small nod. The deputy nodded back and wrote a few quick words in his notebook.

"All right, that's enough of that," he said. "One last question."

"Yes?" said Pamela.

"I hate to even bring it up, but, well, we are on an island. . . ."

"What about it?" said Tam.

Now the deputy looked over toward the pool. Specifically, he looked at the little girl splashing around the shallow end in her water wings. "No chance your son would go swimming?"

"No!" said Pamela. "No, our boy, Davey, he's not a reckless . . ."

"He's not that outdoorsy these days," agreed Tam. "He used to go to the lake when he was younger, but not so much anymore."

"Okay, so you don't think he would, but he'd know how to swim if he did?"

"Yeah, sure," said Tam.

"Exactly," said Pamela. "So it's not that."

Brando thought about it. He remembered asking Davey to go to the lake so many times the summer before, and Davey saying no way. "I don't think he'd go in," he said. But then he remembered Davey before that, Davey diving off the big raft. "I don't think he'd go in far," he added.

The deputy nodded. Brando liked him better now that he was listening to him.

"I think I've heard enough," said the deputy. "I've seen this before. A kid, a teenager, gets to an island like this. Quiet little place. He's going to want some space, and he's going to want something to do. He's going to look to do something. What's he find?

Nothing. There's nothing to do here that early. But there's a boat, and he can get on it for five bucks."

That still didn't sound like Davey to Brando, but his parents were nodding and the deputy had just said he'd seen it before. And Brando liked the idea that Davey could just come back on his own, show up on the next boat. He'd be in some trouble, but he'd be safe.

Marco came pounding over from the walkway. His dress shoes slapped loudly against the concrete as he jogged past the pool.

"Missed it," he said in between huffs and puffs.

"Can you call him?" said Pamela.

"Not on the water. Left a message at the marina. Hopefully he'll get it. Otherwise" — he paused to get more air — "have to wait for the next boat."

"Forget it," said the deputy, standing up. "I'll go run him down."

Brando remembered the sight of the powerful police launch knifing through the water.

"We're going with you," said Pamela.

Tam nodded.

Fulgham considered it. This wasn't even an official missing person case yet. The boy had only been gone for half a day. But it was a good lead, and it didn't seem like there was much more they could do on the island. "Sure," he said. "Boat can take me plus four."

Four? thought Brando. *Sweet!*

"Marco, man, you stay here, all right?" said the deputy.

"No problem," said Marco. His relief at being let off the hook took the form of a dorky thumbs-up.

"Get me the room number of that English dude. You got my number. And have someone put together a list of this morning's checkouts."

"You need phone numbers for them?"

"If you got 'em."

"Sure."

"And Marco?"

"Yeah?"

"If the boy shows, don't let him go anywhere."

26

There were more sharks now. The blue, yes, but two more, as well. The newcomers cruised by in tandem, passing slowly underneath Davey's feet. He watched them closely and followed their progress.

Their fins had black edges and tips. They were blacktip sharks. Davey had seen the little blacktip reef sharks at the aquariums, but he could tell this was a different species, a whole different animal. Each one was as heavy and muscular as an NFL defensive back.

Davey examined their markings with a mix of fascination and horror. They were pure black — as black as their eyes — but uneven, as if each fin had been lightly dipped in ink. The blacktips passed no more than seven or eight feet beneath him. If he hadn't seen them and tucked his legs up, it would've been even closer. *Too close,* thought Davey. Another deep shudder ran through him.

And here came the blue. It hadn't adjusted its course enough, and now it was heading for the same patch of water as the blacktips. Davey watched, the sharks getting fuzzier with distance. He squinted and stared, coaxing his weak eyes to follow them.

Something was going to happen down there. Would they bump into one another? Would they fight?

At the last second, the blue veered off. It shot quickly away, vanishing into the distance. The blacktips continued on, crossing the empty patch of water unconcerned. Davey wasn't surprised. It was small, and they were big. It worked the same way on land. He hoped the blacktips would vanish now, too.

They didn't. They continued on for another dozen feet or so, until they were just a black-and-gray blob in his vision. Then they turned and slowly came back into focus. He pulled up his legs again. In a sense, they'd done him a favor with the blue: a circling shark is never a good sign. It was hard for him to feel too grateful, though, as they passed underneath him again. Closer this time. Not much closer, it's true, but they were in no hurry.

Twenty minutes later, the blue was back. It stayed down deeper, out of the way of the others. Davey could just make it out down there, its penknife body giving it away. It wasn't circling now, just lurking, waiting for the bigger sharks to do the work.

The blacktips passed by again. They were far enough to the side this time that he didn't pull up his feet. He was too tired anyway. The adrenaline that had flooded his system was mostly gone now, and he was crashing. It had been a fight-or-flight response, but he had no way to do either.

The blacktips headed away from him for now, and the blue was almost out of sight. Davey scanned the horizon and then the sky.

Still nothing. He wanted to believe they would find him. It was a bright and nearly cloudless day. The burn on his shoulders was plenty of proof of that. He was a dark dot on a clear sea. A boat wouldn't even have to be that close to see him. A plane wouldn't have to be close at all.

Yes, he told himself, *they'll find me.*

Six feet down, the blacktips arced gracefully and headed back his way.

If there's anything left to find.

27

Davey's aquarium was growing rapidly. The three sharks moved lazily around it, just like the ones back in Cincinnati. And now that Davey was mostly still, the four little fish barely budged from under the water bottle. Even the bright blue fish was back.

And now another one was headed his way. This one was bigger. If Davey had held his hand out flat, with all the fingers extended and together, it would have been the size, and almost the shape, of this new fish. But there was something wrong with it. It was just a few inches below the surface of the water, and Davey didn't even need to look through the water cooler bottle to see that it wasn't swimming right. It flicked its tail in spastic jerks that sent it almost as far sideways as forward.

As it got closer, Davey saw that it never fully straightened out. It always stayed a little curled up, like a dried-out flower petal on a windowsill. He couldn't tell if it was injured or sick or what, but he didn't want it near him.

"Get away," he said.

He didn't even know why at first, and then he did. The sharks . . . He looked at this new fish, struggling its way toward shelter, and all he saw was bait.

"Getawaygetawaygetaway!"

The injured fish kept coming, determined to reach the little island of shade and shelter. Davey scanned the water underneath him. He didn't see the sharks. Where were they? He leaned back, pulling the bottle with him. Slowly, he began to kick.

The other fish came with him. The new fish swam harder, flapping its tail, trying its hardest to go straight. Davey kicked harder. "No! Go away!"

And he was right to be worried. Davey felt the blacktip before he saw it.

A pressure wave of water pushed up against his feet and legs. The shark shot up out of the deep and bit the injured fish cleanly in half. Its momentum carried it up and out of the water, and for a split second Davey saw it there. Half of its thick body was above the water, its wet skin reflecting the sunlight. The rest was still below. Then it tipped and fell back. Water splashed across Davey's face, shoulders, and back.

He swore so loud that he owed the swear jar back in Ohio at least ten bucks.

As the surface of the water began to smooth out, Davey saw the tail of the little fish. Just the tail, still curled, leaking blood and little bits of flesh into the water. The muscles gave one last reflexive flick as it began to sink. Then a shadow, then a shape: The other blacktip surged to the surface. It snatched the scraps. The splash was smaller this time.

Davey kicked harder as the second shark disappeared from view. He hugged the bottle tight to his chest and backed away as fast as he could. He was twelve feet away by the time the blue shark arrived. He saw it thrash back and forth. Its fins broke the surface as it pushed through the bloody water, searching for food that wasn't there.

After a few more thrashes, it gave up. It had been right to stay near the blacktips, but it had been too slow to take advantage. It was too late to get its share. As it left the surface and descended, its primitive brain formed one simple thought.

It needed to be more aggressive.

28

Brando was enjoying the ride despite himself. Back on land, he'd felt angry and sad and guilty all at once. But out here, he could just watch the boat cut the water in half, leaving a wake of white spray.

As soon as the boat began slowing down, his thoughts crept back in. He looked up at row after row of boats tied to a network of floating docks. He'd overheard enough to know that this was the marina and that they were here to look for the captain of the boat that took people to and from Aszure Island. He'd overheard most of what was said on the trip, in fact, because everyone had been shouting over the noise of the engine.

Deputy Fulgham cut the engine and eased the police launch in toward an empty slip. As he did, Brando leaned over the edge and looked down into the vanishing sliver of water between boat and dock. He saw a flash of something on the bottom. It might have been a coin catching the light or a piece of metal that had snapped off the last boat to dock here. Brando would need a closer look to know for sure.

And just like that, he knew what Marco had meant when he

said, "No divers. Please. Not yet." It was so horrible, but so obvious. They would bring in divers to look for his brother's body on the bottom of the sea.

They were talking all around him. His parents were talking to each other. The deputy was talking to someone on the dock. The words were still loud enough for Brando to hear, but his head could no longer hold them. The five words he already had in there were taking up all the space. What did he mean, "not yet"?

Everyone got off the boat and headed down the dock, and he followed them. The concrete-topped dock floated serenely on the water, designed to rise and fall with the tide. They reached another dock that ran parallel to the shore and took a left. Brando finally looked up and saw Key West. The waterfront was bustling with activity. It was the early afternoon, and everyone was on the move.

Brando wasn't even really on Key West yet, but he could hear it clearly. A road ran along the shore. Cars and scooters honked, and bicyclists shouted. And behind that rose the muffled roar of thousands of people on vacation, drunk with sun and possibilities. A loud laugh cut through it all briefly, like a goose honking.

"No way," he said. No one heard him, but he knew it in his heart now. There was no way his older brother would want any part of this. He took a step toward his mom. She didn't have sleeves on, so he tapped her wrist. She turned toward him and leaned down.

"What is it, B?"

"Davey would hate this," he said.

"Okay," she said. "Now be quiet for a second. The policeman is talking."

The deputy was talking to a very short man in very long shorts. "Hey, Victor. You seen Zeke?"

"The Captain? Yeah, of course. He's made a few trips out to Aszure already."

"You been here all morning?"

"Yeah, and I'll be here all day, too."

The deputy took the flyer out of his pocket and unfolded it. "Seen this kid?"

Victor looked at the flyer carefully.

Tam and Pamela leaned in, waiting for his answer. Victor gave them a quick glance before answering. "Don't think so. Tough to say. Lot of kids running around the docks all day."

"Look again."

This time he took the flyer in his hands, but the answer was the same. "Don't think so. Something happen to him? He do something?"

"Just looking for him, that's all," said the deputy.

Victor glanced over at Tam and Pamela again and put it together. "Bad deal," he said to Fulgham. "Hope you find him."

Hope you find him "soon," thought Brando. *He should've said "soon."* But Victor had said what he said. It was another "not yet" for Brando's list.

"We will," said the deputy. Brando nodded in approval. "Where's Zeke now?"

"Probably still eating lunch."

"Yeah, you want to narrow that down for me a little?"

"Oh, sorry. He's at Mary's. Pretty sure, 'cause he asked me if I wanted anything from there."

"Okay, thanks, man."

"No problem. If you got another one of them flyers, I'll take it. Ask around for you, just the people who come and go, you know?"

"Yes, please," said Pamela, stepping forward and handing him a flyer. "We'd really appreciate it."

"No problem," said Victor, taking it in his child-sized hands. "It's a bad deal."

The Tserings followed the deputy to shore like a row of ducklings. He walked them straight off the docks and across the road. He even waved a car to a halt so they wouldn't have to wait for the light. He started up the walkway toward a small, one-story restaurant that seemed to be leaning ever so slightly to the left. The paint was weathered and peeling, hovering somewhere between the dark red it had once been and the washed-out red it was becoming.

"I thought it was Mary's?" said Tam, pointing to a sign that read BAIT 'N SWITCH in slightly fresher paint.

"Mary is the owner," said Fulgham.

Brando slipped by them, pulled open a battered screen door, and stepped inside.

"Hold on there, dude," he heard.

He felt a hand on his shoulder, but he couldn't see who it belonged to. Sunlight streamed in through the windows and door, but apart from that, the only light came from a few signs glowing behind the bar. A man's face emerged from the shadows by the door. What Brando thought at first was a lingering shadow near the man's left ear turned out to be a large tattoo.

"It's okay, Bacon, he's here on official business," said the deputy, stepping into the doorway.

Bacon? thought Brando. *Did I hear that right?* He had, and Bacon straightened up on his stool when he saw the deputy. He pushed a meaty hand through his greasy hair.

"Oh, hey, Deputy," said Bacon. "That's cool. Come on in."

"Glad to see you carding this time. Where's the Captain?"

Bacon let out a raspy laugh. "Gonna have to be more specific. This place is full of 'em."

"Zeke — never mind, I see him."

Brando did, too. He was sitting at a small table with the scattered remains of a BLT spread out in front of him. It was the hat that gave him away.

29

Zeke looked up from his ruined sandwich at the flock of newcomers headed his way. Brando saw his eyes flick across the whole group and then settle on Deputy Fulgham.

"Oh, boy, what'd I do now?" said Zeke. "If this is about last night, I'll tell you right now I don't remember it too clearly."

Brando was pretty sure he was joking.

"Nah, you're not in trouble, Zeke," said the deputy. "At least no more than usual. Wouldn't kill you to answer your phone, though."

"Well, that would be hard, considering there are about thirty feet of seawater over top of it at the moment."

"You drop it?"

"Something like that. How can I help you? Want the rest of my sandwich?"

"Just want to ask you a few questions about this morning."

"Have a seat," said Zeke. He looked around at the others. "You'll have to pull over an extra chair or two."

Tam and Pamela turned to look for empty chairs, but the deputy stopped them. "Why don't you all get some lunch?" he said. "I'll just talk to the captain by myself, if that's okay."

"I'm not hungry," said Pamela.

"Well, get the kid some fries, anyway. They make some mean curly fries here."

"Sure," said Tam, taking the hint. He leaned in and whispered something to Pamela. Brando couldn't hear what it was, but it worked.

"We'll be right over here," she said, pointing to a little square table nearby.

Fulgham nodded. "You can just order up at the bar."

"I'll save our seats," said Brando. He pulled out the chair closest to the other table and didn't knock himself out pushing it in.

The deputy was probably aware of what he was doing, but he didn't seem to care if Brando overheard. "Thought I'd spare you the full inquisition," he said to Zeke.

"I appreciate it. What's this about?"

"Well, that family there is one kid short right now. Thirteen-year-old boy, haven't seen him since last night."

Brando's back was to the deputy. He heard the sound of paper crinkling.

"Here's a picture. You see him this morning, maybe on the first or second boat?"

"Oh, jeez," said Zeke. "That's a tough one."

"Yeah, why's that?"

"Sundays are busy this time of year. Get a lot of checkouts, people who want to be home by Monday."

"Even that early?"

"Yeah, they got flights to catch, out of Miami and everywhere else. Busy on the way over, too. People spend the first night here and then head out to Aszure first thing. Adds up to a lot of people, lot of faces, on that little dock."

"So you don't remember him?"

"Lemme look again. . . . No, I don't think . . . Definitely not on the second boat. I'm a little fuzzier on the first. It was pretty early. Why don't you ask Mar—"

Brando missed the rest of the sentence. His parents had just shown up with a paper cone full of fries. He'd been leaning way back in his chair, and now the front legs clattered back to the ground. The talking behind him stopped.

"Hey," called the deputy. "Mind your own business over there."

Busted, thought Brando. But his parents barely said a word as they sat down, and the deputy didn't lower his voice. The family chewed silently on reheated curly fries and continued to eavesdrop.

"But come on," said Fulgham. "He's a teenage boy. You must keep an eye on 'em. I know I do."

"Yeah, but I don't know. This kid looks young."

"Yeah, his face does, but . . ." The deputy didn't even need to turn around to address the family. "Davey small for his age?"

There was no response.

"Come on, I know you're listening. The fries aren't that good."

"Yes, he's not that much bigger than Brando here," said Pamela finally.

Even with his back turned, Brando could tell they were looking at him. He sat up a little straighter.

"Okay, so he looks young."

"Yeah, well, there were definitely some kids on that first boat, but I honestly don't think he was one of them. And I know he wasn't on the second."

"Yeah, Marco doesn't remember seeing him down there, either."

"What makes you think he took my boat, anyway?"

"Some English guy said he saw him waiting by the dock, early."

"Oh, yeah, that guy. I just brought him back here this morning, him and his family."

"Oh, yeah?" said the deputy.

"Yeah," said Zeke. "Can't miss him. Nice guy, but he nearly sank my boat when he got in."

"They have luggage with them?"

"No, just day-tripping."

Brando and his parents weren't even pretending not to listen now. They'd turned in their chairs and were watching the whole thing.

"Okay, okay, want to do me a favor?" the deputy said to Zeke.

"Do I have a choice?"

147

"Not really."

"Then, yes, I'd love to."

"Take this flyer and show it to the big English guy when he shows up for the ride back. Ask him if he's absolutely sure this is the kid he saw. Just double-check, okay? And then give me a call. Or have someone whose phone is not currently at the bottom of the sea give me a call, okay?"

"He never saw the picture . . ." said Pamela, her words forming along with the thought.

"What?" said Fulgham. "I thought you said —"

"No," she said. "He just said he saw a boy. We assumed. . . ."

"Oh, great," said Fulgham. A shoot-me-now look flashed across his sunburned face as he stood up. "All right, thanks, Zeke."

"No problem. Say hi to the sheriff for me."

"Will do," said the deputy, already moving toward the door.

"We got these to go," said Tam, picking up the half-empty cone of fries.

"Good," said the deputy, "because we're going."

30

Drew looked around, unimpressed. She'd lobbied hard for this trip to Key West, but it wasn't the party she'd been looking for. Or maybe it was exactly what she'd expected, and she was just now realizing that she didn't much care for this sort of party. They were on Duval Street, the main drag. There were some nice shops, and the weather was lovely. But it was also the height of spring break, which meant that it was crowded, loud, and a little crazy around the edges.

"I heard Florida was full of old-timers," said Big Tony, "but this is just a bunch of rowdy yobs."

Drew agreed. They walked past a banner that read SPRING BREAK EXTREMEX. Inside the little building, she could see a bunch of those yobs getting even rowdier.

"What's the extra X for, then?" she called over the noise.

"That's extra extreme, isn't it?" said Big Tony.

Kate didn't answer. Her mouth was fighting a fierce battle against some salt water taffy she'd just bought. "Think I just swallowed half my fillings," she said once she'd finally chewed the piece to death. "Have some of this."

She extended the box to both of them. Drew passed, but Big Tony took two. He began unwrapping both at once. "Don't eat them both, dear," said Kate. "They're different flavors."

Tony looked down at them, one pink and the other light blue. He shrugged. "All ends up in the same place," he said, popping both into his mouth.

"Well that ought to keep him quiet for a while," Kate said to Drew. "What should we talk about then, just us girls?"

Drew smiled, but before she could answer, a group of college kids came barreling down the sidewalk at full speed. It wasn't clear if they were running from something or toward something. Big Tony stood his considerable ground, and the spring breakers either avoided him or bounced off. Kate and Drew shrieked and pressed themselves against the side of a building, narrowly avoiding a collision.

"GRRMMFERRLLS!" shouted Big Tony through the taffy.

"You tell 'em, Da," said Drew.

"What say we get back to our sleepy little island?" said Kate. "Just do some lying about and get some sun?"

That actually sounded really good to Drew. She was a little surprised at herself, but it did. When she got home and Becca asked her about "the party" on Key West, she'd just have to tell her it was a little too "extremex" for her.

She took her phone out of her pocket, just out of habit. The service was switched off — no calls or texts. She checked the time and pretended that's what she meant to do. It was already well into the afternoon.

"Hope that's switched off," said Big Tony, having finally defeated the taffy. "Those roaming charges are bigger 'n I am."

His own phone was back in their suite, switched off, but the hotel phone next to it had been ringing regularly with calls from the police.

Without another word, the Dobkins turned around. They walked slowly back toward the marina. They even crossed the street for some fresh window-shopping on that side of things.

They'd made it almost all the way back to the marina when Big Tony decided to duck into one final store. It was a liquor store, and Kate didn't approve. "They've got a bar on the beach and another one in the hotel," she said.

"Can only imagine what they charge," said Big Tony. "Captive audience and all that."

"Fine, but I'm going in with you," said Kate. "At least we can get something I like, too." She turned to Drew. "You stay out here."

"I'm not going to get legless just walking into the place," she protested. But it was no use. All she could do was post herself by the door as her parents disappeared inside. She watched the world go by, or at least the street. There were sunburned tourists and more college students.

She saw a young copper in shorts go by on the other side of the street. He was scanning the area. She stood up a little straighter as his eyes passed over her. She was standing outside of a liquor store, but there was nothing illegal about that.

She was about to forget the whole thing, but then she saw the family tagging along behind him. They looked familiar, but where had she seen them? It didn't take her long to come up with the answer; it had to be the hotel.

It was that family, that poor family from the lobby. She saw them following the young officer, scanning the street. *They're looking for that boy,* she thought. *But why do they think he's here?*

Tam and Pamela both looked in her general direction, but Duval Street was crowded and they were looking for a thirteen-year-old boy with glasses or a large man with a shaved head. She didn't fit either description, and they'd only seen her in passing at the hotel.

Their eyes washed over her in a big swoop, like the beam of a lighthouse. They kept going. They were past her, and that was just about that. But there was one other person with them, of course.

Brando was bringing up the rear in the search party. It wasn't a lack of enthusiasm; he had the shortest legs. He took one more quick look across the crowded street. A little red car sped by, and when it passed, he caught a quick glimpse of a girl. There was something familiar. . . . A stout cargo van passed, blocking his view. He stopped. He almost got run over by the man walking behind him, but he stayed put. The van rumbled by. It was the girl from the hotel, the daughter of the big British guy.

The guy they were looking for.

He looked more closely, just to make sure. She saw him now: the little boy, the brother. They made eye contact, and she smiled at him. Flustered, all Brando could think to do was wave.

Next to Drew, an elderly lady pushed her way out of the store. Drew helped her with the door and then ducked her head inside. She saw her parents waiting in line at the register.

"Mum, Da," she called.

She'd found something more important for them to check out.

31

Davey was wiped out. It was amazing that someone could be so drained and so waterlogged at the same time. He was cold, his shoulders and head still baking in the sun but his core temperature already down a few degrees from the long soak. He'd been in the water so long, he felt like cold spaghetti.

And he was tired. He'd been hugging the bottle to him since early that morning. Now he'd begun to let go a little. It wasn't going anywhere. He leaned forward onto it, one arm bent loosely around its thin plastic neck. They drifted in a lazy slow dance. Still, his shoulders and arms ached from the constant tension, and his chest was beginning to feel bruised.

But more than any of that, he was mentally exhausted. The sharks, the shocks, the situation, the endless squinting into the distance and listening for any sound . . . They had worn him down like a piece of driftwood. His mind was shutting down, partly to recover and partly to protect itself from the horror of it all.

It was bad timing, because the blue shark was agitated. It was no longer twenty or thirty feet down, avoiding the blacktips. Now it was cutting back and forth in sharp-edged zigzags in the warm band of water between the cruising blacktips and the surface.

It could still smell the injured fish it had missed out on. Traces of blood and the oils from its torn flesh still hung in the current. Now the blue shark was thinking about having a go at this big thing. The blue could sense the electrical charge coming from it and hear the occasional hollow thump of water on plastic. It was an unfamiliar mix. It wasn't a turtle, though it was big enough. The shark didn't know what it was, but it knew how to find out.

A quick bite and then retreat. If it was a tough thing, and dangerous, the other sharks would help tear it apart. The blue had learned that lesson early: There were always more than enough teeth out here. But with something this size, the blue would get its share.

It twitched erratically, making a few last adjustments to its course. The blacktips had seen this sort of thing before and cruised in close behind it. The blue shot toward Davey straight and fast, knifing up through the water at a forty-five-degree angle.

Davey was still leaning forward on the bottle, completely zoned out. Once again, the pressure wave of water arrived before the shark. Something inside Davey stirred. It was the base of his brain, the animal part that had kept him afloat when he was barely conscious that morning. *Danger,* it said. *Wake up.*

He lifted his head and pulled the bottle in a little closer to him. His eyes snapped fully open. There was no time for anything else. The shark was there. Its sleek, pointed nose cut through the last few feet of water. The black eyes rolled back in its head, and its permanent frown widened for the bite, revealing two rows of sharp, serrated teeth.

BONK!

It hit the water cooler bottle.

The impact carried through the plastic and knocked the air out of Davey's lungs. He bounced high enough that the top of his swim trunks broke the surface of the water. The cheap bottle, the plastic a little on the thin side, managed not to rupture. Instead, it bent all the way in and popped back out in midair. Davey held on tight to the top as he splashed back down.

The shark turned sharply to its right and then drifted there for a moment, confused and stunned. It shook its head violently from side to side, part surprise and part bite reflex. But there was nothing in its mouth. Something had gone wrong. It swam away quickly. It understood instinctively that if the other sharks realized it was stunned, they'd tear it apart. That's what it would've done.

The little fish had scattered. If fish could talk, these ones would say, "Ha ha ha! Hit your nose! Loser!"

But the news wasn't all good. The activity had agitated the blacktips, triggering their competitive instincts. And the impact on the empty bottle had created a big sound this time, like a bass drum beating underwater. And big sounds attract big things.

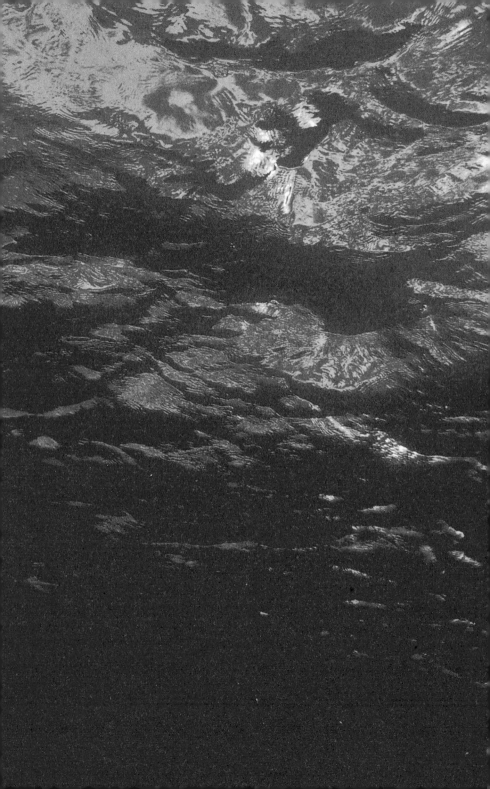

PART THREE

CATCHING HIS DRIFT

32

A misunderstanding that had endured for hours unraveled in a matter of seconds. Standing outside the liquor store on Duval Street, Deputy Fulgham showed Big Tony the flyer. "Is this the boy you saw by the docks this morning?"

"Nah, that's not him." He said it quickly and with a thick accent — *Nah-ats-not-ihm* — but just the initial *N* sound was enough.

Tam shook his head in disbelief, and Pamela dropped hers in defeat. The rest of the Dobkins crowded in for a look.

"No, the boy we saw was younger," said Kate.

"I saw him," said Drew. She reached out and touched the picture with her finger to leave no doubt which boy she meant.

"You did?" said Fulgham. "When?"

Everyone turned to look at her. She took a breath and told them what she knew. "Yeah, that other one, the little one, was just waiting for his family by the dock. I saw him. But this other one, this one here, he was farther on."

"Where was that?" said Fulgham. Everyone was leaning in now, even her own parents.

"Tell 'em, luv," said Kate.

"I was getting to it, wasn't I? He was by the little shed place, the little —"

"The bar stand?" said Fulgham.

"Yeah, that's it," she said. She hadn't wanted to say *boozer.* "It wasn't open yet, but he was sitting under a tree right next to it."

"On the path there?" said Fulgham.

"Little ways back."

Brando spoke up: "What was he doing?" No one else looked over at him or even acknowledged his question, but Drew did.

"He was reading."

I knew it, thought Brando.

Now that she'd answered him, the others started in: Where exactly, what kind of tree, when, and are you sure?

The deputy held up his hand to shush them. "Do you remember what time that was?"

"Quarter to eightish, your time. Maybe a little later, but I don't think it was quite eight."

She looked at her mom, who nodded.

"Yeah, that's about right," said Big Tony.

"Wait, did you see him, too?" said the deputy.

"No, but that's what time we were at that boozer."

Fulgham nodded and scratched another quick note in his little notebook.

"We were at that same place about an hour later, when we first went out to look for him," said Pamela.

The deputy wrote that down, too, before turning to face her. "And you didn't see him?"

"No, and we were there for a while. We definitely would —"

They were interrupted by a pair of middle-aged men wearing matching white hats. "You're blocking the sidewalk!" said the smaller of the two.

Big Tony turned and glared at them both. "I'll block your sidewalk!"

The men crossed the street so quickly that they almost walked into the door of a passing car.

Pamela continued: "And we talked to the guy inside, and he said he hadn't seen anyone."

Fulgham jotted down the new information. "All right, at least that's something," he said. "He was there when you walked by" — he pointed his pen at the Dobkins — "and gone before you got there." He pointed the pen at the Tserings. "Was it an old guy you talked to at the bar stand?"

Brando nodded.

"Old as dirt," said Tam.

"Okay, that's Morgan Bembe — Captain Morgan. I'll need to

talk to him." Fulgham looked around at the bustling street and shook his head. "And we need to stop burning time over here."

"Sorry for the confusion," said Big Tony. "Just trying to help, and I made a mess of it."

"Our fault as much as anyone's," said Pamela.

"Anything we can do to help," offered Kate.

"We may need to borrow your daughter," said Fulgham. "She's the last one to see the boy now."

Kate and Big Tony nodded.

"I'm in," said Drew. "Let's find him."

33

The police launch flew through the water, skimming over the surface and sawing off thick white plumes on either side. Fulgham was gunning the engine and shouting into his radio. The others were mostly just holding on tight. Tam and Pamela were closer to the cockpit, and Drew and Brando were squeezed in farther back.

Drew watched the docks disappear behind them. Her parents were still there, waiting for the next boat.

Brando tried to figure out what this meant. Davey hadn't taken the boat. No one had seen him there, not even its captain. That's what he'd thought all along, but he wished he'd been wrong. Because if he hadn't taken the boat, and he wasn't on the island, that only left —

Drew interrupted his thoughts. "That's your brother, then?" she shouted over the noise. "The one we're looking for?"

"Yeah, uh, Davey," he shouted back. "His name is Davey."

"He likes his books!" She formed her thumbs and fingers into circles and raised them to her eyes: glasses.

"Yeah!" called Brando. "He's really smart!"

"I'm Drew." She leaned over and extended her hand.

"I'm Brando." He leaned over and took it. It was bigger than his, and warm.

The boat bounced over a small wave and they both fell back into their spots. It was too loud to say much more, but Brando felt better now. It was true: Davey was really smart. Even if something bad had happened to him, he'd figure it out.

Drew was just glad Brando didn't look so sad anymore. She wasn't sure what help she could be. She didn't know much more than what she'd already told them. But she was determined to do what she could.

The next thing she knew, the boat was slowing down and pulling up to the little dock on Aszure Island. She braced herself as it bumped to a stop and the deputy threw off the line.

There was a man there to take it, but it wasn't who any of them were expecting. Brando looked around, but Marco was nowhere in sight. The man caught the line and fastened it with a few quick, strong tugs. He was dressed in a dark blue uniform, long pants and a short-sleeve shirt. Brando caught a quick flash of gold from his collar.

Brando thought the man looked like a superhero, and he was half right: He was an officer of the United States Coast Guard.

"That was fast," said Fulgham, hopping onto the dock.

The two men exchanged quick salutes.

"I'm coming from the same place you are," said the man. "At Station Key West all morning."

"Heading back to Marathon?" said the deputy.

"I was." A Coast Guard launch, a little bigger than the police one, was tied up on the other side of the dock.

"Well, I'm glad you're here, Beast."

Beast? thought Brando. Had he heard that right? He had. The man's name was Bautista, but people who could get away with it called him Beast.

Maybe he really is a superhero, thought Brando. Beast was one of the original X-Men, and he was blue, too. Brando didn't even realize he was staring until Bautista gave him a quick smile and snapped off a salute. Brando raised his hand slowly and saluted back.

"I'm Lieutenant Commander Daniel Bautista of the United States Coast Guard," he said to Tam and Pamela as he helped them onto the dock. "I'm here to help any way I can."

Bautista looked over at Brando, whom he'd been told about, and Drew, whom he had not. He didn't want to sugarcoat anything. The island was small and had been searched thoroughly. The boy had been missing for the entire day. That meant he was probably in the water, and that meant he was probably dead. Still, he tried to find something encouraging to say.

"I do have some experience with this sort of thing."

That was an understatement. He was the best they had.

34

Brando understood what had just happened better than his parents did. They'd just been sent away so the grown-ups could talk things over. It happened to him all the time, but it had probably been a while for Tam and Pamela. The "grown-ups" in this case were Bautista and Fulgham. They'd headed off with Drew, so she could show them exactly where she'd seen Davey. The Tserings weren't invited.

The deputy's mood had changed. He was very serious now, and so was the new man, Bautista. He was the one who'd sent them back to the hotel.

Brando broke into a little jog to keep up with his parents. They were headed for the office. People were making phone calls there. They were trying to reach the guests who'd left that morning, the ones who were up early and might've seen something. Bautista said they'd be a big help there. Brando had heard that one before.

They pushed through the back doors of the hotel. The flyers were still up on both sides of the double doors. Davey's face looked out of the paper, a small smile on his lips, oblivious. Tam paused to smooth out the tape on one of them.

"The office?" said Tam to the lady at the front desk. She pointed behind her and didn't protest as they walked around the counter. She knew who they were. There was a little doorway off to the side. It was open a crack, and the buzz of mismatched voices filtered out. The family walked through single file.

One quick look told Brando that they weren't needed. There were two desks, each with a blocky, old-fashioned phone. Marco was sitting at one desk, holding the phone between his ear and his shoulder. "Yes, this is a message for Delmar Granderson. I'm calling from the Aszure Island Inn. I hope you enjoyed your stay! I just wanted . . ."

A man in the same blue uniform as Bautista was at the other desk. Brando knew right away that this was Bautista's assistant, that when you have gold things on your collar, you don't drive your own boat. The man was sitting up very straight in his chair, holding the phone stiffly. He'd left his share of messages, too — many of the former guests were still on planes — but this time he was talking to an actual person. "I see. . . . Of course . . . So, nothing?"

Behind them, another employee was holding a piece of paper, probably waiting for her turn to dial. That made his parents second and third in line, if they even had enough numbers to call.

"I'm going to the room," said Brando.

No response, so he left. There were a few people in the lobby, and they all watched him as he emerged from behind the counter. Maybe they were wondering what he'd been doing back there, and maybe they thought he looked a lot like the boy on all of those flyers.

Brando didn't stop to ask. He went straight to the room. He fished the passkey out of his pocket and swiped it. He waited for the little light to turn green and went inside. The first thing he did was go to the little mini fridge and take out a brand-new five-dollar Coke. He dared them to bill him for it. He twisted the top off the cold plastic bottle and took a gulp so big it almost came out his nose. He wiped his mouth with his forearm and looked around the room.

The beds had both been newly made. The covers were tucked in as tight as ticks about to pop. He raised the Coke to his mouth again. Just before he took another sip, he saw the empty cot. The blanket had been folded into a square, and the pillow had been fluffed and left on top of it.

Brando stood there looking at it. The Coke bottle fizzed away a few inches from his mouth, but he'd forgotten all about it. He'd wanted his brother to get in trouble, to have to sleep on that thing all week. He'd seen it empty and said nothing.

"AAAAAAHHHH!" he yelled at the cot.

His body shook with the effort, and some Coke spilled out and ran down his hand. He looked down at lines of cold, brown liquid and then drew the bottle back like a baseball and threw it against the far wall. The room was still again after that. The only sounds were his breathing and the Coke glugging onto the carpet in the corner. He dared them to charge him for that, too.

He didn't want to be in the room anymore. He walked back to the door and turned the handle, but he let it go again. He walked over to the other side of the room. He pawed through his brother's little stack of books until he found the one he was looking for. *The Hobbit* — he was pretty sure that was the first one. It was the first one Davey had read, anyway. Suddenly, and for the first time, Brando wanted to read it, too.

He tossed it onto his bed, kicked over the cot, and walked straight back out of the room. He wasn't exactly sure where he was going, but he knew it wasn't back to that little office. He walked through the lobby quickly, trying not to look at the people who were looking at him.

"Hey there, hold on," someone said. He was going to ignore them, but something told him to stop and look over. It was probably the English accent.

"Hey, Drew," he said.

"Where you off to?" she asked. Having told them what she knew, she'd been sent to her room, too.

"Not sure," said Brando.

"Hey, let me ask you something," she said.

"Okay."

A couple came through the doors, and Drew motioned him off to the side.

"You're his brother." She was talking more quietly now.

"Yeah."

"So let me ask you: You have any idea where he might've gone?"

"Kind of," said Brando, thinking about it. "Maybe."

"And where's that, then?"

"Somewhere quiet. To read."

"Yeah, right! That's what I think, too. I mean, that's what he was doing when I saw him. Sitting under a tree and reading. Did you tell them that?"

"Yeah, but . . ."

"But what?"

"They didn't listen to me." What he didn't say: *Because I'm a kid, because they think they know better.*

"God, I hate that!" she said, and he could tell she knew what he meant.

A man walked up next to them and unfolded a brightly colored brochure. They took a few steps to the side and spoke even more quietly.

"Do you want to . . ." Drew continued. He could see she was thinking about something.

"Want to what? Go look for him? That's what I was going to do." He hadn't realized it, but as soon as he said it, he knew it was true.

"That's good, but I think we should go find those men."

He nodded.

"That big one, the Coastal Guard, he's . . . different. I don't know, but I think he might listen to you."

"And he's with the deputy," said Brando. The deputy had started to listen to him, at least a little. "Do you know where they are?"

"I know where they were."

"That's pretty good."

"You want to?" she asked again.

Brando had made up his mind. "Yeah," he said. "Definitely."

He started toward the front doors. "Out of our way!" he said to the man hovering with the brochure.

"Hmm?" said the man, still pretending he wasn't listening.

"Not that one," said Drew. She pointed toward the back doors, and they cut across the lobby. They pushed through the doors and past the flyers. They headed out into the light of the slowly setting sun, in search of someone who would listen.

35

Davey was wide-awake again. His nerves buzzed as his eyes scanned the water below him. He'd been riding the adrenaline-rush-to-crash wave all day, and what he had left filled his system. Both his body and his mind were starting to understand that he wouldn't have to do this much longer, one way or the other. If they didn't find him soon, there'd be nothing left to find.

The blacktips were up high now, their fins occasionally breaking the surface. Davey almost liked that. It made them easier to keep track of. With its old territory back, the blue had gone back to circling. The circle was tighter now. Everything was closer to the surface and closer to Davey. The blue's aggression and the blacktips' competitiveness had done that.

The little fish — the four silver-gray and the one bright blue — huddled tightly under the bottle now. Even they sensed the danger in the water.

Davey kicked his feet slowly underneath him. It helped keep him warm and alert. He was also using them as bait. He let them hang down into the water and moved them slowly back and forth.

They were the most obvious targets for the sharks, and he didn't try to fight that. He couldn't watch the whole ocean, but he could watch his feet.

He was so focused on them that a new arrival nearly bumped into him. It was a jellyfish. Its pulpy head pushed to within a few inches of Davey's left arm, which was wrapped around the bottle. He noticed it just in time and kicked himself a little off to the right.

He watched as the thing drifted past, its soft, ghostly head in front and the fine, stinging threads trailing behind. He'd never been stung by a jellyfish. He wondered if it would hurt more or less than a bee sting. But he didn't let himself wonder for very long.

He quickly looked back down at his feet. Nothing. He checked the surface for black-edged fins. Not there. He peered through the bottle again. After a long, bad minute, the blue circled back into view. He located the blacktips a moment later.

He let himself relax, just a little. He had no way of knowing that a much larger animal had slipped into a wider orbit around this little aquatic menagerie. He wanted another look at that jellyfish. It was such a weird creature. The light passed through it. The tentacles moved like curtains in a summer breeze. It could be a creature in *The Lord of the Rings*, straight out of the Sundering Seas. He wondered if J. R. R. Tolkien had ever seen one. Did they have them in England? Or maybe when he was in the army, in the First World War?

He reluctantly took his eyes off it and went back to his grim watch. Thinking about Tolkien had opened something up in him, though. He was looking down into the water, but his thoughts were a thousand miles away. He thought about home. He thought about seeing *The Hobbit* in the Cineplex and knowing before it was even over that he needed to read the books. All of them. He remembered his mom taking him to Joseph-Beth Booksellers and the haul of treasure he'd returned with.

And then he remembered taking that treasure and locking himself into his bedroom with it, as if he lived in the dark and doomed Mines of Moria. Why had he done that again? It seemed so dumb to him now. He had come to understand one thing very clearly during his time in the water: Being alone, truly alone — it sucked.

If I was home again, he thought, *I would take the first book to the living room table and read them all through right there. Mom and Dad would be just through the archway in their office, and Brando would be over on the —*

"Ow!" he said.

He felt a sharp pain on the back of his leg.

The first thing he thought was that he'd lost track of the jellyfish and it had stung him. He looked down into the water behind him. He was blinded by a momentary glare on the surface. When it cleared, he knew he was wrong.

He saw two things. The first: a shape disappearing down and away. The second: a little red cloud, wafting up through the clear water.

It was blood, his own this time.

36

It felt good to be running. Drew and Brando had been tagging along behind their parents all day: asking permission, moving at the speed of grown-ups. Now they were ready to get a move on.

"This way," said Drew, waving Brando over to the right.

"Where are we going?"

"The dock! That's the last place I saw them."

As soon as Brando knew where they were headed, he sped up. He passed Drew, but only for a moment.

"Oh no you don't," she called. She sped up and passed him back. She had longer legs, but was wearing flip-flops; he had shorter legs and sneakers. It was a pretty even race, and they were neck and neck when they reached the dock.

"Not here," huffed Brando.

"Doesn't look like it," puffed Drew. The two launches bobbed on the little waves on either side of the dock. The last time she'd been here, the two men were in the larger one, using the radio. Both of them were empty now. The dock was deserted except for a family of three, sitting on their suitcases, waiting for the next boat.

"Should we ask 'em?" she said.

"You do it," said Brando.

"You shy?" she said, and that did it. Brando marched right out onto the dock. She waited on the sand, catching her breath.

"They said they went that way," he said, pointing down the walkway that led toward the far side of the island.

Drew nodded and then reached down and slipped off her flip-flops. Brando knew he was in trouble now. He took off running. For a good ten seconds, all he could see was the open path in front of him. Then he saw Drew coming into view out of the corner of his eye. He leaned forward and ran even harder, but it was no use. Once he saw the soles of her feet, he knew he had no chance. On the plus side: It took them no time at all to catch up with Bautista and Fulgham.

"There they are," said Drew. She went from a run to a walk in the space of a few strides. Brando slammed on the brakes behind her and just avoided a collision.

Bautista and Fulgham were standing just off the walkway, looking out over the water. Now they looked over. Fulgham leaned in and whispered something to Bautista.

"Yes?" said Bautista.

After running flat out to find them, Drew and Brando suddenly realized that they had no idea what to say.

"Um," said Brando.

Drew gave them a weak wave with the hand that wasn't clutching her flip-flops. She felt a little dumb holding them, so she knelt down and put them back on.

"This isn't really a good time," said the deputy. That was putting it nicely. The island was too small and the boy had been gone for too long. The fact that they'd basically been chasing their own tails all day made it that much worse. "Do you have something to tell us?"

Drew pointed to Brando.

"Um," he repeated.

"Something besides 'um'?" said Fulgham.

Bautista was a little more patient. He'd just arrived, after all. "What's your name?"

"Brando."

"And you're Davey's brother?"

"Yeah."

"And is there something you'd like to tell us?" He wasn't, when it came right down to it, that much more patient.

"Um . . ."

Fulgham leaned over to say something else to Bautista. Before he could, Brando blurted out, "I knew Davey didn't take the boat!"

Fulgham gave him a look somewhere between *Now you tell me* and *Thanks for throwing me under the bus*. But Bautista was more curious. "And how did you know that?" he said.

"Because he's not like that."

"Like what?"

"Davey, he doesn't like, like, loud stuff."

"No?"

"No. He, um, reads a lot, up in his room. Like a not-normal amount. And he took his book with him. His favorite one."

"And he wouldn't go to a busy place like Key West to read a book," said Bautista.

It wasn't really a question, so Brando didn't answer. But Drew added, "And when I saw him, he was sitting under a tree and reading."

"So he found a quiet spot here," said Fulgham, the annoyance gone from his face.

"But then people start walking by," said Bautista.

"And it's not so quiet anymore," said Fulgham. "So . . ."

"He goes to find somewhere that is."

Bautista looked over at Brando and Drew. They both nodded: *Yes, exactly.*

"So, any ideas where he would find a place like that?" said Bautista.

"Whole island's pretty quiet, especially at that hour," said Fulgham.

"Yeah, but we're talking alone-in-his-room quiet," said Bautista. He turned to Brando. "You were all in the same room, right?"

"Yeah. He had the cot." He wasn't sure why he added that last part.

"Right, so he's thirteen, crammed into a room with his whole family, wants some me time . . ."

"There's a roof deck," said Fulgham.

"I was up there, right after we got back," said Drew. "He definitely wasn't there."

"Okay," said Bautista, looking out at the band of sand between the walkway and the water. "What about the beach?"

"People there, too," said Fulgham. "Morning walks on the beach . . . It's a thing."

"Right, right," said Bautista. He'd forgotten about that; it wasn't a thing in the Coast Guard.

Everyone was quiet for a few moments. The only sound came from the small waves and the gulls. Finally, Brando spoke up. "There's a little beach," he said.

"What do you mean?" said Bautista, but Fulgham already knew.

"Oooh yeah," he said. "But you went there, right? Marco said —"

"Yeah," admitted Brando. "We looked around a little."

"And?"

Brando just shrugged.

"What are you . . . ?" said Bautista.

"Little beach, at the end of the island, kind of cut off," Fulgham explained. "It's definitely secluded. People can get a little carried away out there because —"

"Carried away?" said Bautista.

"I didn't mean . . ."

Bautista looked over at Brando, then took another quick look over his shoulder at the water. "Think it's worth a second look?"

Fulgham thought about it. It was a small beach, and it had already been searched. But searched by whom? An upset, untrained family and the hotel manager.

"Might as well," he said.

Brando let out a long breath. Drew looked over at him. "I think this is good," he said.

"Aces," she replied.

They headed straight down the walkway. It wasn't far, and in just a few minutes they'd navigated the narrow path and arrived on the little beach.

"This is nice," said Drew.

Brando looked around. Everything was the same as this morning, except two ladies were sunbathing halfway down the sand. They looked up and saw two men in uniform and two kids in shorts.

"Is it okay to be here?" called one.

"There was no sign," called the other. "Except for that." She pointed to the sad little NO SW MM NG sign.

"No, no, you're fine," called the deputy.

The ladies dropped their heads and went back to catching rays. Bautista had missed the whole exchange. He was walking slowly across the sand and staring straight out at the water.

"Oh no," he said.

"What?" said Fulgham, but then he saw it, too. "Son of a . . ."

"What?" said Brando. He looked out at the water, but all he saw was, well, water.

"Please tell me that's not what I think it is," said Bautista.

"No, I think it might be."

Both men started jogging toward the water's edge. Then they started running.

"What are they after?" said Drew.

"I don't see anything," said Brando.

"It's not . . ." began Drew. She couldn't bring herself to say *a body*, but Brando read the word in her silence.

"I don't see anything!" he repeated.

They took off at a run, too. It was no race this time. There was a bad feeling in the air, like they'd already lost. They caught up with Bautista and Fulgham at the edge of the water.

"Well, I guess we know why that sign's there," said Bautista.

"It's completely inadequate," said Fulgham. "Gonna write about eight citations."

"Make it a dozen," said Bautista. Then he began to walk out into the breaking waves, shoes, long blue pants, and all.

"What's he doing?" said Drew.

Brando had no idea, and then he saw it. The water was higher and the waves were bigger than they'd been that morning. The larger ones tucked themselves into neat little barrels as they broke. They were bigger everywhere, except where they weren't. Where

183

the rip current was cutting them down. Bautista waded diagonally into the stretch of flatter water off to their left. The waves hitting his knees there were little more than bumps on the surface.

Drew saw it now, too. She watched as he waded out a few more steps. He stood still there for a moment, then quickly turned and headed back toward shore. He was a big, strong man, but she could see he was working hard. He was powering his way to shore.

Fulgham saw it, too, and walked toward the water to give him a hand.

"Stay there!" Bautista said. He grimaced and pulled his legs forward through the shallow water.

"The sea is *pulling him*," said Brando.

Drew could hear the horror in his voice.

A few more powerful steps and Bautista broke free.

"Something must've shifted out there," said Fulgham. "Think there's a sandbar. If it'd been this bad for long, someone would've noticed."

"I'm afraid someone might've," said Bautista. He pulled a blocky device from a sheath on his belt. He pressed a button and got static back. "Akers, you copy?" he said. Brando remembered the Coast Guard man in the hotel office.

The big walkie-talkie crackled. "Yes, sir. This is Akers, over."

"Yeah, I need you to get down to the boat and patch me through to Marathon, ASAP."

"Now, sir?"

"Yes, now. Get it!"

"Roger that, sir. I'm gone!"

He turned to Brando and Drew. "Which one of you is the fast-est runner?"

Brando pointed to Drew. It didn't hurt his feelings or wound his pride. He was glad she was so fast. Right now, he wished she had wings.

She reached down and slipped off her flip-flops.

"Get back to the hotel and get everyone off those phones and back here. Lead them straight here, to this beach, yourself. I don't want any more confusion today. I don't want any more wrong turns."

He cast his gaze around the edges of the beach. "We're going to turn this place upside down," he added, but Drew was already gone.

37

Davey had been bitten by a shark. It shouldn't have been that surprising; he'd been surrounded by the things. But it was. It honestly kind of blew his mind.

It was a treacherous little nip. The blue shark had tried the direct approach and failed. So it approached slowly and cautiously on the second attempt. It wormed its slender body up through the water behind Davey and gave the back of his right calf a quick bite, just to see what sort of thing this was. Sharks don't have hands, after all. If they want to know what something is, they bite it.

Two rows of sharp teeth punched through Davey's skin, creating connect-the-dot half-moons on either side of his lower leg. Then the blue let go and quickly swam off. It didn't clamp down hard and shake its head back and forth to tear off the meat. This was just a test. It knew there'd be plenty of time for feeding later.

That time had arrived. The blue cut in between the blacktips, emboldened by the blood in the water. The larger sharks swam farther apart and then back together, but they kept coming. They were all converging on Davey.

He pushed the mouth of the water cooler bottle below the surface, allowing some seawater to funnel in. The little fish that had been beneath it were long gone. They smelled the blood, too, and knew to get clear. The bottle sank lower as the sharks got closer. They were close enough to the surface that he didn't need the bottle to see them. Plus, it was his only weapon.

The reality was overwhelming, so he tried to frame it as fantasy. He pretended that the blue was an orc and the blacktips were trolls. The bottle was his wizard staff and sword both. The blue arrived first, and he pushed the bottle forward. It was heavier now that it was partially filled.

BLEHNNK.

It was a slow, glancing blow. The plastic brushed against the shark's gills. It recognized the thing from before, remembered the impact. It veered off to the side. The tip of its long, flat pectoral fin scraped the bottle as it went. And it didn't go far.

Davey located the two blacktips and tried to square the bottle up between them. If they split up, he wouldn't be able to block them both. He had to hope they wouldn't. As he watched the midnight tips of their fins slice through the surface toward him, a new fin rose into sight.

It was fifteen, maybe twenty, feet behind the blacktips. It rose up through the water and kept rising. It was six inches high, then a foot. Davey's eyes were weak, but a bat could've seen the massive shape moving toward him under that fin. This was no orc; the Uruk-hai had arrived.

The blacktips were almost on him. Reluctantly, he shifted his focus back to them. But they never arrived. They sensed the weight and power of the thing behind them. They were as big as pro athletes; the tiger shark was as big as a boat.

Davey wasn't even surprised when the blacktips veered off and dove down. He knew by now that blacktips were a timid, curious sort of shark. He knew just by the fact that he was still alive.

But they knew what they were doing. They would wait for the scraps.

38

They were spread out across the beach. Brando and Drew were working the tree line like monkeys. Pamela had walked all the way to the edge of the beach on one side, and Tam had made it all the way to the other. Marco was pulling a garden rake across the sand in long rows. It wasn't clear what he thought he'd find that way, but he was working hard at it. Sweat dripped from his forehead, and dark stains blossomed under the arms of his dress shirt.

The other hotel employee from the office was walking back and forth across the sand. Even the two sunbathers were doing their part, standing at the edge of the surf and looking out into the water. Deputy Fulgham stood nearby, shielding his eyes with his hand and scanning the horizon. "I should really go back to the launch and get my binoculars," he said to Bautista.

Bautista wasn't listening. He was talking to the Coast Guard station at Marathon. The one at Key West was closer, but he was stationed at Marathon. The radio in his hand had been patched through the more powerful one in his boat.

"I can't confirm anything right now," he was saying. "But that's what it's starting to look like."

And then someone started shouting and everything else stopped. It was Brando. He knew how his brother squirreled things away. He'd seen it many times: money and keys hidden under a hat under a shirt under a towel at the lake; his glasses tucked behind the ladder leading up to a waterslide.

By the time Fulgham and Bautista arrived, Brando was already walking back out from the scrub brush at the edge of the beach. He was crying softly. He had a book in one hand and a pair of glasses in the other.

Drew didn't know what to do and just stared at the glasses. Marco threw the rake down into the sand. Tam and Pamela converged from opposite sides of the beach at dead runs.

"Oh my God," said Pamela.

"No," said Tam. "No."

But there was no denying it anymore, and the two went to pieces after that. Bautista raised the radio back to his mouth. He spoke loudly and clearly so that he could be heard above the sound of it all.

"Station Marathon, this is Lieutenant Commander Bautista. You read me?"

There was a burst of static and then the response: "Roger that. This is Coast Guard Marathon. I got ya, Beast."

He took a deep breath in, pushed it out, and then pressed the button.

"What do we got in the air?"

*   *   *

Things happened fast after that. Above them, returning from an uneventful law enforcement patrol, an HC-144A Ocean Sentry radioed in. Lieutenant Commander Chris Abelson confirmed the surveillance plane's position and received his new orders.

"Search and rescue," he repeated. "Roger that."

Up at Air Station Clearwater, Lieutenant Amy Vandiemas had the rotors of her MH-60T turning. She shouted back at one of her airmen to stop moving around. Then, in a practiced, even tone into her headset: "Flight controls are checked. . . . Instruments are checked. . . . All checked." And the big helicopter lifted into the sky.

Back on the island, Fulgham was approaching the dock. His feet were as blurry as a hummingbird's wings as he pounded down the walkway. Behind him, Drew and Brando were doing their best to keep up. It was very clear that Fulgham didn't plan to wait.

Bautista was at the edge of the little beach, trying to reassure Tam and Pamela. "We'll do everything we can," he said.

His eyes scanned the water. Akers was bringing their boat around. Bautista could hear it coming now and waited impatiently for it to appear. Once it did, Bautista strode back out into the water. He grabbed the side and hauled himself aboard. Before his legs even cleared the gunwale, Akers pushed the throttle down.

39

The only reason Drew and Brando made it onto the police launch was that Deputy Fulgham had to navigate through the people waiting on the dock and then spend a few moments casting off the line. When Drew hopped aboard, he spent a few more moments telling her she really shouldn't be there. During that time, Brando hopped aboard, too. The boat was already drifting away from the dock, and Fulgham gave up.

"Fine," he said. "Just put those life jackets on and hold on tight!"

They snapped the vests on and hunkered down as he pegged the throttle. He honked his air horn twice as he zoomed past Captain Zeke's fat-bottomed boat. He carved a wide white semicircle in the water as he swung the launch around and headed toward the far end of the island.

Fulgham was pretty sure they were wasting their energy, but he had to try. If the kid was still alive, they didn't have much time. He'd been at sea far too long already. And if he wasn't, well . . . The body would either get hung up on the bottom and picked clean or would wash ashore on its own. Either way, he'd want to know — he'd *need* to know — that he'd tried his best.

Brando watched the shore until he saw the little beach come into view. He saw his parents' backs as they headed toward the path. Then he turned and began scanning the water. "I'll watch this side," he called over to Drew. "You watch that one!"

"Right!" she said, but she was already doing it.

Fulgham eased off on the throttle as they came up on Bautista's boat, which was floating almost motionless now. Brando looked over and saw Bautista throw something over the side. It was an orange ring with a blinking beacon attached. Drew watched it splash down. It caught the current immediately and began to drift away from the boat.

Fulgham cut his engine, and everything was suddenly quiet. For a few moments, everyone on the water was just watching the orange ring float away. Finally, Bautista broke the spell. "We're right on top of the sandbar," he shouted over. "You go on ahead! I'm just going to take it slow back here. Don't want to over-shoot him."

"Got it!" shouted Fulgham. Then he stepped back into the cockpit and hit the throttle.

Brando and Drew looked at each other as the spray kicked up around them. They knew what it meant. Fulgham had to risk zooming right past Davey. He had to take the chance to try to get there in time. Brando leaned out, his eyes open as wide as he could get them. They were covering water fast, just eating it up at this speed. He scanned the surface, looking for his brother, looking for anything.

Drew did the same, taking her eyes off the water just long enough to check the time on her phone. It was almost six.

Fulgham was thinking the same thing. "I don't like this," he was saying into his radio. "Too long to stay afloat without a life jacket. And that sun's going to go down. . . ."

Bautista was listening in on the other end. He knew what it meant. Once the sun went down, hypothermia would set in. And there was something else. Bautista lowered the binoculars from his eyes briefly and looked down under the surface of the water. *Dawn and dusk,* he thought. *That's when the sharks like to feed.*

But three miles away, the sharks weren't exactly watching the clock. The big tiger shark was bearing down on Davey. It was close enough now that he could see the faded stripes along its back. He had no idea what to do. This thing was blunt-nosed, thirteen feet long, and twelve hundred pounds. It was like a truck coming at him with bad intentions. He gripped the plastic water cooler bottle, but it just felt flimsy and pathetic in his hands.

For a moment, he thought maybe he could swim for it. The shark was moving slowly. But then he remembered: Swim where?

He had nowhere to go. And he was pretty sure the shark could move fast if it wanted to. He was right about that.

He watched, horrified. The thing was five feet away . . . four . . . three . . . He pushed the bottle forward and down. He wanted to get more water into it, to make it heavier.

BLUHMP BLUHMP

Water rushed in and fat air bubbles rushed out.

Two feet . . . one . . .

BLUHMP BLUHMP

This was it. He could see the shark's teeth now. He was close enough that he could see the serrations along their edges. He would be torn apart, mashed and sawed. He pushed the bottle forward at the thing. He was right, it was far too flimsy and light to stop so massive an animal. But the bubbles . . .

BLUHMP BLUHMP

They confused the shark. They hit its nose and slid across its skin. There was a faint, distasteful scent of sunbaked plastic and an odd gurgling sound. The big tiger veered past with a sudden burst of speed.

It brushed by the blue shark, which had slipped around behind Davey again. The smaller shark skittered away.

But once again, neither shark went far. Davey's leg continued to bleed, to bait the water, and they both circled back.

The bottle was heavy in his hands. He'd let too much water in.

Instead of lifting him up, it was dragging him down. The last few bubbles of air slipped out. He kicked hard and tried to lift it out of the water, to dump it out like he had before. But the strength he'd had then was gone now, all spent, and then some.

It slipped from his hands and disappeared. He honestly thought about following it down. It seemed so much more peaceful than being torn apart, eaten alive. But he didn't. He was a quiet kid, but no quitter.

He lifted his head out of the water and took a deep breath. The air seemed delicious to him, and he took another quick breath. He was greedy for it in the way you suddenly want something that's about to be taken away from you.

There was a droning in his ears now. He assumed it was his racing pulse, but his pulse couldn't get any faster and the droning was getting louder. He looked up just in time to see the HC-144A. The drone turned to a roar as it zoomed low overhead.

Treading water now, Davey turned and watched it go. A yellow flash caught his eye as something fell from the plane. Before it even hit the water, orange smoke began pouring from the little canister.

Like the sharks, the plane began to circle around. Unlike the sharks, though, it couldn't reach Davey. The Ocean Sentry is a surveillance aircraft, not a seaplane. Lieutenant Abelson did what he could: "Be advised, we have an update on person in the water." He read off the location, advised the other searchers of the smoke canister, and then added, "We need to hurry on this one. Looks like he's not alone down there."

The smoke signal landed fifty yards away, a good shot if you think about it. Davey swam for it, keeping his eyes on nothing but the billowing orange smoke. The tiger swam slowly after him, with the blue in its wake and the blacktips angling in from the other side.

Of the other searchers, Fulgham was closest. The deputy had overshot him, but not by much. He could just see the smoke now, like an orange cotton ball in the distance. The throttle was all the way down and Fulgham was stomping on the floor, kicking his launch like it was a lazy horse. Brando and Drew held on tight, trying not to get bounced out of the boat as it crashed through the late-day swells.

Davey didn't hear him coming. He barely had the energy to lift his mouth out of the water between strokes. His muscles ached from clutching the bottle all day. His lungs burned and his pulse pounded. Pain shot through his injured leg as he kicked it weakly through the water, but he kept going.

He was moving slowly and had made it a little more than half-way to the smoke by the time the police launch arrived on the scene. Deputy Fulgham saw the splashing first, and then the boy who was causing it. He was amazed that this kid was still on the surface, much less still swimming.

He aimed the boat right for him, but had to cut back on the throttle so he'd be able to stop in time. And then he saw the fins:

dorsal and caudal, and big, very big. He knew it was a sea tiger. It was right behind the boy.

"Oh no," whispered Fulgham.

His hand went to the gun on his hip, but he didn't draw it. He wasn't sure it would stop the thing, and they were a protected species anyway. Tiger sharks might attack a few people a year, but people had killed thousands of them in these waters, just for the sport and the fins. Instead, the deputy got back on the throttle and drove the launch right toward the thing's dorsal fin.

The shark heard the powerful engine getting closer and felt the vibrations shake the water. These were no little bubbles this time. It veered off and dove down. Fulgham let out a long breath.

Drew and Brando had spotted Davey now, too, and arrived at the cockpit.

"Was that a . . . ?" Brando began before swallowing his stupid question. Of course it was a shark.

"Get him quick! Get him quick!" said Drew. She grabbed the orange life ring hanging on the side of the cockpit, but it wouldn't come loose.

"Okay, okay," said Fulgham. He reached over and unclipped it. "I'm going to pull up alongside him, and you toss it to him. Throw it in front of him — don't hit him with it!"

Brando ran over to the side of the boat. "Davey!" he called. "Davey, we're here!"

Davey saw the boat now and changed course toward it. He saw his brother standing on it and waving, but he thought there was a good chance he was hallucinating that part. The boat cruised slowly toward him, and he swam for it. *Please don't let me die now,* he prayed, *not when I'm so close.* He saw the English girl he'd seen that morning, holding a big orange ring. *Yep,* he thought, *I'm hallucinating. Please at least let the boat be real.*

Fulgham edged it slowly forward. He flicked his eyes from Davey to the water around him, scanning for the tiger shark. He knew he'd shoot now if he had to. Drew did the same thing as she waited to toss the ring.

"Come on, Davey!" shouted Brando. "Get out of there, man! Get out of the water!"

What do you think I'm trying to do, Hallucination Brando? he thought.

The boat was close enough now. Fulgham cut the engine, and Drew tossed the life preserver. Davey took a few big swings at the ring and finally got his right arm over and through. Drew tugged him to the edge of the boat. Davey pushed the life preserver aside and grabbed on to the side of the boat with both hands.

Drew reached down and grabbed his right hand, and Fulgham hopped past her to get to his left. Everyone scanned the water. There was still no sign of the big tiger shark. But no one was looking for that sneaky little blue.

The smaller shark surged forward below the surface and clamped on to Davey's leg, harder this time. It swung its head to the side with surprising power and pulled Davey out of Drew's grasp and clean off the side of the boat. Davey's head dipped under the water, and a mouthful of seawater slipped into his lungs.

"Son of a . . ." said Fulgham. His hand was still extended, reaching for a hand that was no longer there. He could see the blue now, a few feet down and clamped on tight. He grabbed for the gun on his hip, but he never got the chance to use it.

Brando took two quick steps, jumped high up in the air, and then tucked himself into a tight ball. He plunged down into the warm, clear water and landed on the blue shark's back.

It was at exactly that point that he realized: *Holy cow, I just cannonballed a shark.*

The blue wasn't much happier about it than he was. This floating thing was a tough meal to get! Reluctantly, it let go. Brando felt its sandpaper skin scrape across his shins as it slipped away. He opened his eyes in time to see Davey pulled onto the boat. His legs disappeared, leaving only a red cloud in the water. A red cloud that Brando was now in the middle of.

As he bobbed back toward the surface, his eyes registered a huge darkness, approaching him like a thundercloud rolling in. He burst into the air, already grabbing for the side of the boat. Two arms reached for him, two hands just a little bigger than his own.

Drew pulled hard. She refused to let go and leaned back as far as she could. Brando's chest cleared the side, and then his hips. Only his legs were still in the water. He kicked frantically.

He looked into Drew's face. His eyes said *Please please please* and *Hurry!*

Drew gave one last tug and fell backward.

Drew's butt hit the deck, and Brando's legs cleared the water.

Fulgham saw that he was aboard, grabbed a towel, and turned back to Davey. The white towel turned red as the deputy pulled it tight around Davey's lower leg. Davey grimaced and then coughed up more seawater.

"Is he?" said Brando

"He'll be fine," said Fulgham, not looking up. "He's lost some blood. We just need to get him to shore."

Brando nodded. "He can have my bed," he said.

Fulgham had no idea what he was talking about. But Davey did. *That really is my brother,* he thought. Despite the pain and exhaustion, he smiled.

Drew heard a noise and looked up. Bautista's boat was easing up next to them. Overhead, she could just hear the first faint sounds of a helicopter's rotors. She looked back down at Davey and shook her head in wonder. *This boy was carried away by the sea,* she thought, *and the world has come to carry him back.*

40

The sun set over the ocean, and that was fine because Davey wasn't in it. He was lying in a clean white hospital bed with fifty-six fresh stitches in his leg. They'd done a lot of work in the little hospital on Key West. Cleaning the wound, cutting away the dead flesh, stitching him up. They'd knocked him out for it, but it was hardly necessary. After it was over, he slept straight on till morning.

For the second day in a row, he'd woken up to the sight of an unfamiliar ceiling. And now, a few hours later, he found himself once again crammed into a small room with his entire family. But they weren't snoring this time; they were talking.

"It's like a Bengals game out in the waiting room," said Tam.

"Browns!" said Brando. He had — in classic Brando fashion — chosen his own team. Two days ago, that was exactly the sort of thing that would've started an argument. Not now.

"It's like a Bengals-Browns game," said Pamela.

Tam and Brando smiled; those were always good games.

"Who's out there?" asked Davey. "Who's waiting?"

"Lots of people want to talk to you," said Tam.

"Like who?" said Davey. Images of state police, FBI agents, and possibly his school principal flooded his mind. He was still having a hard time believing that he wasn't in trouble for causing so much commotion.

"Reporters, for one," said Pamela. "You're big news."

No FBI agents, but that wasn't much of a relief. The thought of TV cameras and tape recorders — of having to explain himself — made him nervous. "Who else?" he said.

"Your aunt from Miami," said Pamela.

"I didn't know I had an aunt in Miami," said Davey. He looked over at Brando for confirmation. He shrugged.

"You *don't*," said his mom. She opened her eyes wide with fake fear.

Davey laughed. He must be big news to bring reporters and crazies to the same hospital.

"Yeah," said Tam. "We might keep that one waiting a while."

"How about forever?" said Brando.

Davey chuckled again. He looked down at the spot where his right arm emerged from under the hospital gown. It was badly burned from a full day of direct sun and devilish glare. He reached up with his right hand and poked a particularly wicked patch just below his shoulder. All he felt was a weird tingle. And now that he thought about it, why didn't his leg hurt more? He couldn't see what was going on beneath all that gauze, but they'd told him about the stitches.

"I'm pumped all full of painkillers, aren't I?" he said.

"Oh yeah," said his mom.

"Big-time," said his brother.

"What if I get addicted?"

"See, that question right there is why you won't," said his mom.

He looked over at the IV bag. It was hanging from a metal hook above his bed. A long plastic tube hung down, ending in a needle that disappeared under a strip of white tape on his left arm. "They're in there?" he said.

"Yep," said his dad.

"What else?"

"Just salt water and some antibiotics, I think."

"Salt water?" he said. "I think I've had enough of that already!"

It wasn't a great joke, but once they started laughing, they didn't stop for a long time. It was pure relief. When they finally stopped, Davey had something else to say. He almost chickened out, but he couldn't. Out on the water, he'd made a promise to himself: If he ever got the chance, he'd say it.

"I missed you guys."

The room was quiet now. It was his mom who spoke first. "It must've been so lonely out there."

He looked at her. They realized at the same moment that he didn't mean he'd missed them "out there," or not only that. He meant before that, too; he'd meant up in his room. Davey looked down, his blush hidden by his sunburn.

"We missed you, too." It was so quiet, barely a whisper, that Davey wasn't even sure who'd said it. It could have been any of them, and that was enough for him.

Someone knocked on the door: three firm raps. Tam straightened up and muscled a smile onto his face. "Ready for the first group of visitors?"

"Not the reporters!" said Davey.

"No," said Tam. "They can wait." He got up and went over to the door. When he opened it, one man filled the entire frame. Davey recognized him from the morning before: the big British guy.

"Thanks for coming," said Tam.

"Wouldn't miss it," said Big Tony. The room seemed smaller as soon as he entered. He was followed by the rest of the family.

"Hi, Drew!" said Brando.

"Hey, B-Boy," said Drew.

Just like that, Davey knew his little brother had a new nickname. Drew pushed Brando in the shoulder in place of a handshake. Then she turned toward the bed, where Davey had something else he'd been waiting to say.

"Thank you."

Drew had expected the words, but not the emotion behind them. All she could think to say was, "It was nothing."

All Davey could think to say was, "It wasn't."

Then suddenly the whole room was talking. Davey leaned back. Brando — or was it B-Boy? — started telling everyone about chasing after Deputy Fulgham and hopping into his boat. How Fulgham hadn't really wanted them there. How they weren't about to ask. After that, he did a spot-on impersonation of "the Beast." Everyone laughed. Davey lay back and listened. He felt lucky to have a brother like . . . well, like whatever his name was now.

And then, as if she was reading his mind, his mom said, "We were lucky."

"How's that, then?" said Big Tony.

"Lucky you were there on that street, that you took the boat you did."

"Oh, that was her idea," he said, hooking a thumb at his daughter.

Drew smiled shyly, slightly embarrassed by what she was about to say. "I thought this was where the party was."

"Yeah," said Brando. "The search party!"

The whole room laughed again, louder now, because there were more people. A few minutes later, a nurse came in with a fresh bag of IV fluid and the Dobkins were ushered out of the room. Brando walked Drew to the door. Big Tony, who'd been first in, was last out.

"I'll see you back on the wee island," he said before ducking out the door. "Business meeting and all that. Hope you don't mind I didn't bring a tie."

"Not one bit," said Pamela.

"I might make one out of a palm leaf," said Tam.

"What was that about?" said Davey once the room was quiet again.

"Oh," said his mom, "well."

Davey waited her out.

"All right, well, it turns out that he works in imports. . . ."

Davey turned to his dad for confirmation. "Thinks there might be a big market for Tibetan goods there in England. As long as they're authentic."

"And of the highest quality," added his mom.

Davey looked at them both. They were wearing cat-that-ate-the-canary smiles that made him smile, too.

"Ready for the next group?" said his dad.

"The reporters?" he said.

"Afraid so. Can't keep them out there forever."

Davey shrank a little further into his bed.

"Don't worry," said Brando, stepping forward. "I can be, like, your spokesman."

Davey sat back up. "Okay," he said. He couldn't think of a better guy for the job.

"Shake on it?" said Brando.

It didn't seem like the kind of thing that required a handshake, but Davey leaned forward anyway. And when Brando reached over and grasped his hand, he understood. His little brother held on tight.

They both did.